Marcus turned his head at the gentle sound of the opening door and came to his feet before he fully appreciated the vision that stood on the stairway.

For a moment the power of speech was reft from him. It was forgivable. In that moment Fleur was incredibly lovely. The gaiety of her smile curved her lips and the knowledge that she looked better than her best kept her head high. Yet there was a half-enquiring, mischievous tilt to that proudly held head that made her vivid little face wholly enchanting. Only the childishly slender arms betrayed the fact that she was not yet fully grown to womanhood.

And in that brief, dazed moment, Marcus caught his first glimpse of the woman she might become. "And I thought her less than pretty!" he remembered in self-scorn. "She is lovely. Radiant. Exquisite."

"My lady," said Marcus very formally, and swept her a magnificent bow. "My very sovereign lady."

MARRIAGE ALLIANCE

Mira Stables

A FAWCETT CREST BOOK

Fawcett Publications, Inc., Greenwich, Connecticut

MARRIAGE ALLIANCE

THIS BOOK CONTAINS THE COMPLETE TEXT OF THE ORIGINAL HARDCOVER EDITION.

A Fawcett Crest Book reprinted by arrangement with Robert Hale & Company

ISBN 0-449-23142-9

Printed in the United States of America

10 9 8 7 6 5 4 3 2 1

For Tom and Molly Gyte

ONE

"Am I required to express appreciation for the courtesy of this visit?" demanded Lord Blayden acidly. "It cannot be more than two months since I sent an express to your lodging, saying that the matter was urgent."

Such a greeting would have intimidated most men, but Marcus was inured to his father's ways. Indeed, his friends occasionally told him that his resemblance to his sire was too close for comfort. Moreover, he was perfectly well aware that it was no more than a month since his father had sent for him. He did not even blench. "I have been out of

Town," he said indifferently. "As soon as I had your letter I came post."

"And think to hang the expense of it to my account," snapped his lordship, "your pockets being, if I mistake not, wholly to let, as usual."

His son smiled but did not answer. When his father was in this mood it was better to let him vent his feelings unchecked.

"And it means nothing to you," Lord Blayden continued, "that in the meanwhile I have been obliged to tolerate the encroachments of an impudent upstart of a tradesman who, in a better organised state of society, would never have ventured to approach me."

Now *this was* a new departure. Marcus knew that his father's pride of race was insufferably inflated. In Lord Blayden's reckoning there were not half a dozen members of the nobility who could match him in terms of pedigree. Nor, indeed, in the extent of his debts, thought his only son wryly, unless it be the late Duchess of Devonshire. Nothing would ever persuade him that society did not owe the ninth Baron Blayden a life of effortless comfort, whatever his financial standing. And to do him justice, his tastes were almost ascetic. He ate sparingly and drank surprisingly little in an age of heavy drinking. His appearance was neat rather than modish. But everything about him, from his handkerchiefs to his horses, must be of the first quality. A foible that his estate could easily have supported had it not been for his passion for gaming.

In his early manhood he had been, reputedly, a devil for the petticoats, but that had come to an end with his marriage. He had been a faithful husband and a just parent, even if a stern one. Nor had the loss of his wife at the birth of their daughter driven him to seek consolation in the arms of a mistress. Instead he had sought distraction in cards and dice and racing, plunging ever more deeply, with varying fortune and little sign of emotion whether he won or lost.

When it was discovered that the puny baby who had been hastily baptised Deborah would go lame all her life because of a hip injury sustained at birth, Lord Blayden received the news with unimpaired calm. The brat was being fed and tended. It might or might not survive. Neither then nor later did he show any sign of affection for the sickly infant who had been the unwitting cause of his loss, but then, neither had he shown any for his only son. He plunged once more into his over-riding preoccupation and was rarely to be found at home.

So it was that Marcus came to develop a fiercely protective tenderness for his little sister. Left so much to the care of servants, the two lonely children had clung to each other. When Marcus went to school, Deborah cried herself into a fever. Eagerly they looked forward to the holidays. For each of them the other signified all that they knew of home.

Maturity brought longer separation. Marcus inherited a small Kentish manor from the uncle who
had been his godfather. The place was too small to
justify the employment of a steward and he came
to spend a good deal of his time there whenever his
other engagements permitted, discovering in himself, rather to his surprise, the makings of a true
countryman, wholly absorbed in the nurturing of his
acres. Deborah, now a schoolgirl in the charge of a
succession of governesses since her delicate health
made boarding school ineligible and no one would
stay long in the isolation of Blayden, was perforce
left behind. But the old affection still linked the
two. They corresponded regularly, and when his
father's peremptory summons had finally reached
him, Marcus had obeyed it the more willingly because now he would see Deb again. If she could be
pronounced strong enough to endure so long a
journey, his father might even consent to her returning with him to pay a visit to Dakers, his
Kentish home, which she had never seen.

Meanwhile it behooved him to enquire into the
cause of that summons, since his father seemed to
be in no hurry to enlighten him and was still ani-
madverting bitterly on a state of society which permitted gutter-bred cits to rub shoulders with
noblemen of countless quarterings just because they
chanced to be gold inlaid, while undutiful sons
lingered over their own pleasures, thus exposing
their sires to all the unpleasantness of toad-eating,

crude attempts at patronage and insufferable boredom.

Marcus preserved a grave front in the face of this catalogue of hardship. "I will spare you my sympathy, sir, since it would be ill-informed," he said gently. "Who *is* this gentleman who has put you to such discomfort? I do not recall the presence in the neighbourhood of anyone answering to this description when last I was at home."

"Gentleman!" snorted his fulminating progenitor. And then, remembering his situation and his plans for meeting it, made a visible effort at a more temperate tone. "As to that," he said stiffly, "being an older man, I daresay he would not have come much in your way, though he has rented High Barrows these ten years past. And now that underbred whelp, young Vernon, has sold to him. Says it's to meet his father's debts," he concluded in an unwilling grunt.

Instinct warned Marcus that they were approaching delicate ground. The Willerbys of High Barrows were one of the few families whom his father accepted as near equals. Old Robert Willerby had died a year past, having exceeded man's allotted span in spite of a career given over to every form of extravagance and excess. It was not in the least surprising that his son should find himself compelled to sell High Barrows— and lucky if the proceeds of that sale paid off the load of debt. He himself would almost certainly have to sell Blayden— unless, indeed, his father was compelled to do so

first. Two seasons in London under the aegis of a
parent who had felt it to be his duty to sponsor his
son into the "ton" had left Marcus with no illusions
about the possible value of his patrimony. If the
older man had been deliberately bent on dissipating
his fortune he could not have been more ruinously
reckless. Marcus had a pretty good notion that the
sudden summons to present himself in Cumberland
had its impetus in financial difficulties. Probably
he was to be asked to consent to the breaking of
the entail. The wealthy merchant of whom his
father had spoken so disparagingly might well be a
prospective purchaser for the faded grandeur that
was Blayden, though what he could want with it
when he already had High Barrows was something
of a puzzle. Perhaps he needed some of the outlying
farms to round out his estate or even to create a
park. Such trappings of gracious living were much
valued by the newly rich, he understood. Honest
farm land would not content a man of that type. He
composed himself to listen with what patience he
might.

But it was not until after dinner, a meal served to
the two of them in lonely state since Deborah was
confined to her room with a migraine headache, that
Lord Blayden brought himself to embark upon his
disclosures. Sliding the port decanter towards his
son and glancing keenly at him under knitted
brows, he said abruptly, "Leg-shackled yet? Or in
the way of it?"

"Good God, no, sir! What should I want with

a wife—even if I could afford such a luxury, which I can't. Believe me, I go on very comfortably without."

There was the faintest discernible relaxation in his father's pose.

"Then I've a proposition to put to you," announced Lord Blayden. "Not to wrap things up in clean linen, it's low tide with me. In fact, it's worse than that—it's a damned drought. The devil's been in the bones of late—cards, too. I shall come about, of course. It's just a matter of raising the ready until the luck turns, and that's where you can help me, if you're agreeable."

Quite illogically, Marcus was moved to faint pity. It must have cost the old man a deal of effort to get that out. "The entail?" he asked. "I'm quite willing to compound with you. Settle things just as you think best."

This generous response met with a sad rebuff. "Break the entail?" demanded his father incredulously. "Are you mad, boy? What good would that do? Even if I'd consider it—which I never would. The place is mortgaged to the hilt. The price it brought would be swallowed up immediately and I should be left without a feather to fly with. No. The scheme is better than that."

He fell silent. Marcus watched him closely. They were approaching the nub of the matter and he scented danger.

"This fellow Pennington," said his father slowly.

"The new owner of High Barrows?" asked Marcus quietly.

Lord Blayden nodded. "Devilish plump in the pocket," he jerked out. "Able to buy an abbey—or a husband of rank and breeding for his granddaughter."

It was out in the open now, and worse than Marcus had imagined. His lean, hard-bitten face, so like his father's, was normally schooled to a tolerant imperturbability, but for once revulsion was written plain about the lines of the harsh mouth, disgust clouded the heavy lidded grey eyes.

His father said, "It's not the kind of match I'd have planned for you. But you're not in the petticoat line—said so yourself, just now. And Pennington would come down mighty handsomely, apart from making the wench his heiress. The blood's common —no use denying that. Yeoman stock on the sire's side, which is bad enough, and some finicking French musician or dancing master on the dam's, which is worse. But there's wealth enough to gild the pill."

Marcus could scarcely believe that he had heard aright. His father's affairs must be in a shocking state if he was even *considering* such an alliance. But one thing was sure. So far as *he* was concerned, he would have none of it. He was quite unsentimental about it. The marriage of convenience was part of the social fabric in which he had been reared and he saw a good deal to recommend it where there was community of interest and background and a degree of liking between the contracting parties. But such a match as his father proposed was a very different matter. Marry an unknown female of plebian origin—for he was sufficiently his father's son to curl up his high-bred nose at *that*—simply in order to finance his father's gaming? No! Not even to save the home of his ancestors would he consent to such degradation. He strove to master his sense of outrage so that he might couch his refusal in such terms as should not cause a permanent breach between them.

Lord Blayden had not expected instant acceptance of his preposterous proposal, but he was determined that it should not be rejected out of hand before he had pointed out all the advantages that would accrue from its achievement. He did not give his son a chance to speak.

"If you can bring yourself to accept the blood lines, you've swallowed the worst," he swept on imperiously. "The rest is simple. The girl is young and has been reared to strict obedience and submission. Her husband will have no trouble with *her*. There is nothing in her appearance or her manners to give you a disgust of her and she seems to be healthy and well-formed." He had almost described her as being apt for breeding, but something in the frozen distaste on his son's face warned him to go warily. He hurried on, to avoid any possibility of interruption, "But there can be no delay. It seems that the girl's mother—the Frenchwoman—is still alive. Pennington is obsessed with the notion that

she may yet turn up to claim the wench and interfere with his plans for her. So he is determined to
have her safely tied up in wedlock without loss of
time. Which is why I wrote to you that the business
was urgent," he concluded.

Marcus was aware of a brief flash of pity for
the unknown girl, a helpless pawn in the hands of
strong-willed and unscrupulous men. It seemed to
him unbelievable that her own grandfather was
prepared to bestow her on a man of whom he knew
nothing save that he would inherit a high-sounding
—and empty—title. Of his own father's conduct
in the business he preferred not to think. Cold-
hearted he had always been, but Marcus had not
dreamed that he could be so callously selfish.

He roused himself to break the strained silence
that had fallen as his father's voice ceased.

"What made you imagine that I would lend myself to such a scheme?" he said quietly.

Lord Blayden took this for encouragement. At
least it was not the immediate and downright refusal that he expected.

"Necessity," he said bluntly. "I have realised all
my disposable assets, pared my expenses to the
bone. Only a desperate remedy will serve to redeem
the situation now."

Marcus accepted the statement as truth. "Put
the place up for sale, then," he urged again. "Cut
your losses. There is still the Town house. In any
event, you already spend most of your time there.

And if Town air doesn't suit Deb, she can come to me."

"And how do you propose to support yourself and your sister? By your agricultural endeavours?" demanded Lord Blayden brutally. "Your allowance —a mere pittance, I am aware, but useful none the less—derives from Blayden's rent-roll. It will cease when Blayden goes under the hammer. Your place in Kent is little better than a farm. I doubt if it is adequate to support *you,* let alone a sickly girl who must be cosseted and sheltered from any hardship."

There was truth in that, too, harsh, unpalatable truth. For himself he could make shift to live on the fruits of his labours, even if he must forego the allowance that his father had always made him. But he could not take risks where Deborah's health and comfort were concerned. Dakers was beginning to thrive under his fostering care, but it had been long neglected and it would be two or three seasons yet before it would be really soundly established. He could sell it, he supposed. But to do so would only briefly stave off the inevitable, while throwing away all hope of future security.

They seemed to have reached point non plus. But he was still determined that neither necessity nor persuasion should win his consent to his father's scheme.

"Such a marriage as I propose need not affect your present way of life," pursued Lord Blayden. "You may leave your wife here. Your little manor could not house her fittingly, you will explain, and she will be a companion for your sister. You may go your own way with an easy mind. Pennington will not complain. As I judge it, he cares nothing for the girl save as a means of establishing that foothold in society of which her father cheated him."

Marcus swallowed his disgust at the heartless words. "Her father?" he raised an enquiring eyebrow.

"Oh! *He* was to have been the corner stone of the Pennington rise to social eminence. The father is quite unlettered, but he had had the boy well taught and got him into one of the mercantile banks. Money, you see, will pave most paths. But he disobligingly fell tail over top in love with this Frenchwoman—a penniless refugee. Married her secretly—afraid of his father—and died of the lung fever when their brat was still in the cradle. It all came out then, of course. As I understand it— though I paid scant heed to the fellow's maunderings—he pensioned off the mother and undertook to rear the child. Now he is wholly set on seeing her wedded to the future Lord Blayden—and willing to pay handsomely for the privilege."

"If that is all he requires, let him content himself with the present holder of the title," said Marcus shortly. "*You* are a free agent, sir. Marry the wench yourself."

"And I gave you credit for a degree of common sense," sighed Lord Blayden with weary patience. "How would *that* serve the fellow's purpose? If I were to marry the girl and, perchance, get brats on her, you still stand to inherit the title."

Marcus had had enough. "Then Mr. Pennington had best set about seeking some other title for his heiress," he said curtly. "If he is so wealthy, he will have little difficulty. Indeed, I wonder at it that he should have been content to settle for a mere barony. An earldom at least should be his goal. For my part, I had rather die unwed—and the title with me."

There was a painful silence. Lord Blayden's expression was inscrutable as ever. Presently he said, almost idly, "Your last word?"

Marcus inclined his head.

His father shrugged slightly, and spread his hands in a gesture that would have done credit to Pontius Pilate. "A pity. When you are older you may be a little less nice in your requirements. Ah well! Nothing else for it. It will have to be Deborah."

Marcus's dark head came up with a jerk. "Deb?" he exclaimed. "How does *she* come into it?"

"She doesn't," said his father. "But I must find some way out of my difficulties and since *you* are in no mind to be helpful, Deb is the answer." There was a brief, pregnant pause. Then "Maxwell has offered for her," he finished gently.

If Marcus had sickened at his father's proposals anent his own marriage, this suggestion filled him with murderous fury. Despite himself, his fingers curled to a stranglehold, his eyes blazed pure hatred. Maxwell! The fellow's name was a byword for every

form of lechery and vice. Older by several years
than Lord Blayden himself, he had buried three
wives and the count of his lights o' love was legion.
There were darker murmurs, too. Hints of perver-
sion and cruelty so vile that the simpler folk made
the sign against the evil one when they chanced to
cross his path. Maxwell—and his fragile little sister!

There was a mist before his eyes and sheer rage
choked his utterance. Through the pounding of the
blood at his temples he heard his father's voice
say smoothly, "She has grown to be quite a pretty
creature in spite of her disability. But at two-and-
twenty I never thought to receive an offer for her.
However, it seems that Maxwell chanced to see her
on her way to church and was much taken with her.
He is prepared to make a very handsome settlement," he ended pensively.

Somehow Marcus managed to contain his fury
and speak soberly, though the hoarseness of his
utterance betrayed the strain under which he
laboured.

"You cannot be serious, sir. Maxwell—and my
sister! Why, I would not trust him with a dog that
I was fond of. Far less a human being!"

"Oh, come, my boy! You make too much of it.
To be sure his reputation is not of the best, but
rumour was ever a lying jade. No doubt it is exaggerated. As his wife, Deborah will enjoy every
luxury that his wealth can command. And he is
even wealthier than Pennington. A man of culture,
too. He was so kind as to say that Deborah put him

strongly in mind of some female of Roman times. Now what did he say she was called? Ah, yes! I have it! Lucretia! Shakespeare, he said, wrote of Lucretia's purity and beauty. A pity that I am not scholar enough to recognise the reference."

And *that* was a lie, thought Marcus, who recognised the reference all too well. His father was laughing at him. "You cannot do it, sir," he insisted impetuously. "You—her father."

The air of calm enquiry on Lord Blayden's face was answer sufficient. His rage broke bounds. "You're reckoned to be a fair shot," he said savagely. "Better to put a bullet through her. It would be kinder."

"But less profitable," pointed out Lord Blayden simply.

Wild thoughts of having some eminent physician examine his father with a view to having him put under restraint came into Marcus's mind, only to be dismissed. Save for this one warped and twisted facet of his mind he was as sane as any man. There were even those who would contend that in disposing of his daughter's hand to a man of wealth and position he was perfectly within his paternal rights, despite the prospective bridegroom's age and unsavoury reputation.

He thrust back his chair without ceremony and began to prowl up and down the room. "Does Deb know of your plans for her?" he shot at his father, thinking that here, probably, lay the cause of the headache that had prostrated her.

"But naturally," his father said, eyebrows a little lifted in surprise. "She was startled, of course. Perhaps a little overwhelmed by the honour done her, she having lived so secluded. I did not press her to give her suitor an immediate answer. I do not think they have even so much as met, though naturally she knows him by repute. But I do not doubt her readiness to oblige me in this. Like Miss Pennington, she has been well instructed in filial obedience."

The deliberate mention of the Pennington girl reminded Marcus that there was still *one* way in which he could save his sister from the nightmarish horror of marriage with Maxwell. A way which, however reluctantly, he would take if no other escape offered.

"I must see Deb. Talk with her," he said abruptly.

"By all means," rejoined his father politely. And as his son flung angrily out of the room, permitted himself to smile reflectively into the ruby heart of his wine glass. The business was proceeding better than he had dared to hope. Deb's pitiful revulsion would assuredly take the trick.

TWO

THE schoolroom at High Barrows had never been remarkable for comfort or charm. Mr. Pennington having decided that only females or menials would use it, had caused it to be furnished with the minimum of outlay. He was not one to squander his blunt where the results would go unnoticed. But since he, himself, never set foot in it, deeming that his new consequence required that all his dependents should wait upon *him* when he chose to summon them to his presence, the shabby room attained a status of its own as sanctuary. The dining-room and parlours in all their garish opulence might be the setting for hours of social endurance, the library the scene of painful reckoning; the schoolroom on the second floor of the west wing was a haven, where loud, hectoring voices did not penetrate. Insofar as these were ever attainable to those subjected to Mr. Pennington's whims and tyrannical temper, it represented peace and safety.

Since Fleur had been sent to school the room had gradually been denuded of the small homely objects that once had softened its ugly outlines. The books had been packed away, save for a much beloved and sadly tattered volume of Perrault's tales that shared the top of the pianoforte with a pile of music. The pianoforte that Grandpapa had insisted upon buying. The room might be bare and dingy, but there was money enough and to spare for anything that might add to her social accomplishments, and since she had no aptitude for singing or for sketching in water colours she should learn to perform on this new-fangled and extremely expensive instrument.

Maman, already a talented performer on spinet and harpsichord, had loved it, but to Fleur the lessons had been burdensome, the necessary practice a drudgery, even though she loved the music and could listen contentedly for hours when Maman played. Nowadays the pianoforte was rarely opened. Grandpapa had abandoned hope of turning his plebian duckling into a social swan. The painstaking practice of studies and sonatas was spared her, and for that, at least, she could be thankful.

There was no great deal to be thankful for,

thought Fleur gloomily. Not since Maman went away. Dutifully, as she had been taught from babyhood, she reminded herself that she should be thankful to Grandpapa for a comfortable home and a good education. Had it not been for his generosity they might have starved to death. But starvation, to a little girl who had never gone hungry, was only a word. And Grandpapa, who was bad tempered and a bully, shouted at Maman and made her cry. So how *could* Fleur love him, even if it *was* her duty to do so?

But there had been weeks and blessed weeks when Grandpapa was away on business, and then Maman and Fleur could be happy together, though quietly, for fear that someone should tell Grandpapa about their foolish gaiety. Once he had stayed away for a whole summer. It was their second summer at High Barrows. In the unaccustomed freedom from constant criticism, Maman had grown quite brave. That was when she had arranged for the long mirror to be hung in the schoolroom and had persuaded the estate carpenter to fix a barre along one wall so that Fleur might do her exercises properly. It was perfectly understood between them that, in case of enquiry, the mirror was necessary for the practice of proper deportment, while the barre was hung with writing copies or the sampler that Fleur was stitching to make it appear educationally desirable.

For the dancing was their special secret. Grandpapa would be furious if he knew of it. Maman had never dared to tell him that she had been an opera dancer for several months when first she came to London. It was not at all a proper thing for a lady to be, but what would you? One must eat! And at the time Maman had not known that it was improper. Such things were regarded differently in France. Maman was only sixteen, and at the ducal court where she had grown up her dancing had been much admired. How she had been proud when she had been permitted to dance in the ballets that her papa had arranged and produced for the Duc's guests! But in England, it appeared, things were quite different. In England, being an opera dancer meant that ill-conducted gentlemen were at liberty to tease and pester one with unwanted attentions. That was how Maman had come to meet Papa. Not that *he* had been one of the badly behaved gentlemen, of course. But he had chanced to walk down the street when Maman was trying to hold off the advances of a horrid creature who, overcome by wine and admiration, was insisting that she accompany him in his carriage to a 'snug little nest' where he would undertake to prove his devotion by such lavish entertainment as the little lady had never dreamed of. Papa had given this unpleasant person something known as a 'leveller'. Fleur did not know what that was, but it had persuaded him to cease from distressing Maman with his importunities and Papa had escorted her back to the humble lodging that she shared with Grandpère.

Maman, in fact, in her desperate loneliness, had

talked a good deal more to her small daughter than was either seemly or prudent. But since they had only each other to talk to, no harm was done. And so long as Fleur had Maman for her constant companion, she, at least, was perfectly happy. Maman was gay and amusing. She had a fund of wonderful stories of her life in France before the Terror had driven her father to take the desperate step of fleeing to England—a flight dictated mainly by his fears for the safety of his precious only daughter.

In England they had fallen on hard times. Their small store of money dwindled rapidly and London was crammed with refugees, many of them of distinguished family, all of them only too eager to give lessons in music or dancing or painting—anything that would earn them a few sous for food and lodging. M. Lavelle managed to find one or two music pupils, but such work was poorly paid and, truth to tell, he was not very good at it. Without capital to purchase an interest, there was little hope of finding an opening in the world of ballet production. But at least his careful training had enabled his daughter to find employment. The ballet was becoming increasingly popular. Perhaps his little Martine would achieve fame and fortune. She had undoubted talent and had been well taught from babyhood.

Those dreams had ended with Martine's marriage, but in their place he had the comfort of knowing that her future was assured. Alexander Pennington seemed to him an estimable young man.

He was in a good situation and well able to provide
for a wife and family. Moreover he was perfectly
willing to house his father-in-law. Life went on very
comfortably in the bright little house in Hans Town.
Alexander was even able to put M. Lavelle in the
way of meeting one or two people in the theatrical
world who might help him to find an opening for
his talents. The future had promised fair, especially
with the birth of his grand-daughter, Fleur. Martine was more settled with the coming of the child.
Her feeling for her husband was no more than a
gentle affection grown out of gratitude. It was not
that undying passionate fervour of which the poets
sang, but how many people, thought practical M.
Lavelle, could hope to find *that* in marriage? His
son-in-law seemed well content with his pretty doc-
ile wife and Martine adored her baby. It was more
than many people ever achieved. He had a shrewd
suspicion that Martine's young heart had been
given, once for all, to one who had probably
perished on the guillotine with the rest of his family.
In any case, nothing could ever have come of *that*
affair. Young Paul de Trèvy had been drawn into
their circle only through his passionate love of
music. A delicate young man, a distant connection
of the late Duchesse, he had been employed in some
secretarial capacity in the ducal household because
his disability—he had a club-foot—rendered more
active occupation ineligible. He had been carelessly
kind to Martine—the unthinking kindness of a
sweet-natured young man to a charming child. He

had taken a friendly interest in her progress, given her one or two small gifts—a box of bon-bons—a perfume sachet—a riband for her hair. In return Martine had bestowed upon him the innocent adoration of her fifteen-year-old heart. Fate had intervened to separate them. And just as well, thought M. Lavelle, since nothing but heartbreak could have come of his daughter's love for one so far above her. No. She was better as she was. Though he wished that Alexander would summon up the courage to tell his father of his marriage. He had planned to do so if the child had been a boy, trusting in his father's satisfaction at the birth of an heir to the Pennington name to overcome his annoyance that his son should have married a girl who had neither rank nor fortune to recommend her and was a Frenchwoman to boot.

Alas! The marriage had not been blessed by the much desired son. Instead, when his daughter was but two years old, Alexander Pennington had died, and his father, outraged and furious at the deception that had been practised upon him rather than grief-stricken by bereavement, had descended upon the pleasant little house in Hans Town to see for himself the wife and child of whose existence he had first learned from his son's will.

A young man at the start of his career, Alexander had had little to leave apart from the house. He had commended his wife and child to his father's care. Mr. Pennington proceeded to issue edicts which Martine was too subdued to question. She and the child were to live with him and all decisions as to the rearing and education of his grand-daughter would be his. She might endow her father with such moneys as Alexander had bequeathed to her. Properly invested, the sum would bring in a tiny pittance which would make it possible for him to eke out a living if she allowed him the use of the Hans Town house in addition to his scanty earnings. His fierce energy had dominated the bewildered household and he had swept off his two hapless de-pendents to his grim establishment on the outskirts of Leeds before Martine had recovered from the shock of her husband's sudden death.

Fleur could just remember the Leeds house, but most of her childish memories were centered on High Barrows. Not all of them were unhappy. Until she was twelve there had always been Maman. Maman, who played with her and taught her her lessons and her music and, above all, her dancing. Daily practice, said Maman, was the secret of good style. And without good style, even pronounced talent would not suffice. Then she would tell Fleur of the beautiful ballets that she had seen, and dance snatches of the various rôles as she described them, until the child was caught up in a worl of enchant-ment far remote from the bleak Cumbrian fells that surrounded their new home and the squat looming shadow of Grandpapa.

But the nymphs and goddesses, the princes and magicians were only figments of Maman's creating. Grandpapa's dour presence most effectively banished them. And it was Grandpapa who put an end to the idyllic days of childhood by his announcement that Fleur was to go to school. He had secured a place for her at a very select seminary in Harrogate. It was time, he said, that she should learn to support the character of a lady and to mix with damsels who would be her contemporaries and her rivals in the marriage mart in a few years' time. For once Maman forgot her fear of him and found the courage to oppose this decision, appealing against the threat of separation and begging that, if her own simple accomplishments were judged inadequate, a governess might be employed to instruct Fleur at home.

"Don't be so daft, woman," grunted Grandpapa with his customary courtesy. "It's not book learning the lass needs. She's going to school to rub shoulders with the nobs and learn how to go on in society. She can't learn *that* at home."

There could be no further appeal. Grandpapa's word was law. In due time, Fleur went to school.

She found it tolerable. She was not exactly happy, but it was new and interesting and she looked forward eagerly to the holidays when she would be able to tell Maman all those details that she had sense enough to omit from the carefully scrutinised letters that she dutifully penned on alternate Sunday afternoons. So it was deeply disappointing to be told that Miss Melling was to accompany her on the journey to Cumberland and would spend the holiday at High Barrows. Miss Melling was one of the junior governesses and Fleur liked her well enough, but she did not want anyone to share the precious hours of the holiday with Maman.

But those precious hours were to be wholly denied her. The mounting anticipation of the last weeks at school, the hours spent in painstakingly hemming a handkerchief for Maman's present, the long miles of the journey home in the new and gleaming carriage that Grandpapa had sent for them, the race of eager flying feet up the grand staircase to Maman's room—all to end in desolation. The room was empty. Not only empty, but swept bare. It held no breath, no faint lingering perfume of Maman's presence.

Millicent Melling had done her kindly best to soothe and comfort the terrified sobbing child; had tried to hearten her, after that devastating interview with Grandpapa. Of course her mother would come home again. She had only gone on a *visit* to her own papa in London. Why! She might even now be on her way, delayed, belike, by bad roads or some minor mishap. Fleur had listened and tried to believe the encouraging words. But in her inmost heart she had known, from her first glimpse of the bare little room that once had been so warmly, fragrantly feminine, that Maman would never return. It was with no surprise that she received, a few months later, a curt message from her grandsire announcing that her mama—he had always insisted on the English form—had married again. "Some Frenchman with whom she was acquainted before her flight to England," said the letter. At least he had told her the truth, she thought drearily. No more need for anxious wondering about Maman's fate, since now she had a husband to protect her. No more room for hope that one day Maman might return to High Barrows. It seemed that she had no further need of her daughter's love, since she had not troubled to write to that daughter. Fleur was still only a child and saw everything as black or white. She could not envisage Maman's feelings, left alone in a household that she had always felt to be hostile, bereft of all that had made life worth living, until she had felt that she must escape and had taken the impulsive decision to visit her father. Nor could she guess at the strange encounter with the past that had awaited her upon arrival. She felt herself discarded and was almost inclined to sympathise with Grandpapa's pronouncement that Maman had no further part to play in her life and that from now on she must look to him for all her needs.

To do him justice, in material ways, he had made ample provision. Though she was a sad disappointment to him, he had done his best for her. But despite her expensive education and every advantage that money could buy, nothing would turn Fleur into the image of his dreams. That she was not bookish he found forgivable—after all, no one really admired clever females. It was harder to accept her lack of ladylike accomplishments, especially when he recalled the money he had spent on their attainment. But worst of all, she was such a plain little piece. Mr. Pennington's notion of feminine beauty was something delicately pink and white, with big blue eyes and winsome dimples and a prettily rounded figure. His grand-daughter bore no resemblance at add to this delight-picture. In fact, with her thin, immature body and ivory wedge of a face with its enormous shadowed eyes, she looked more like some starveling from the slums, as he frequently assured her. But he was, he claimed, a fair-minded man, and he grudgingly allowed that his grandchild possessed two admirable assets. She carried herself like a princess, with a lovely, fluid serenity that stemmed, had he but known it, from the daily practising instituted by Maman and still faithfully followed by her daughter. And on horseback she was the finest and the pluckiest little rider that ever he had seen. Mr. Pennington, who had come late in life to equestrian exercise, was not much addicted to it himself. He was not sure that Fleur's performance was strictly ladylike, shrewdly suspecting that a more restrained and timid bearing would better beseem a female. But the tough fighting spirit in himself which, together with a shrewd brain, had raised him from humble beginning to his present position of power and affluence, recognised and saluted the courage that informed his granddaughter's slight frame, and though he could not bring himself to commend her in words he saw to it that she was well turned out and superbly mounted.

Her horses—and Melly. And soon there would be

no more Melly. The young governess was to be married at Easter. She was very sorry, she said, to desert her charge, whom she held in genuine affection, but now that her Philip had at last been presented to a living he needed her support and it would not be right to ask him to wait. Since they had already waited six years, during which time Melly had spent most of her holidays at High Barrows, no reasonable person could cavil at that. But Fleur was going to miss her dreadfully. Now that she was done with school, the days seemed endlessly long. Despite Grandpapa's wealth—perhaps, even, because of it—they had never been wholly accepted into the social life of the neighbourhood. Very few invitations came her way. Nor had she made any close friendships at school, thereby once again disappointing Grandpapa's expectations. The shock of Maman's desertion—for although the years had brought more understanding, Fleur still accounted it desertion—had made her chary of bestowing too much affection on any one person. It was better—safer—to be on terms of easy friendship with a number of her schoolmates rather than risk a closer intimacy that might end in further bitter hurt.

When Melly went she would be alone indeed. And of late Grandpapa had stopped talking about the arrangements that he proposed for her debut. Perhaps he had given her up as hopeless and did not intend to squander any more money on trying to turn her into a society lady. Which was disap-

pointing, not because she cared so much for the
promised delights of the social round, but because
she *did* long to visit London. That was only natural.
She had been born there, and Maman had talked so
much of the house in Hans Town and of Grandpère, of theatres and concerts and the Opera, that
Fleur felt that she knew them all and longed to see
them. And secretly she hoped that somehow she
would be able to get in touch with Grandpère, if
he was still alive, and hear news of Maman. Perhaps, when Melly left, the London scheme would
be revived. Grandpapa *could* not desire her to spend
the rest of her life in seclusion at High Barrows.
And since he had little liking for her society—she
was too much like Maman—perhaps he would
make a determined effort to launch her on the
marriage market.

THREE

THINKING of Maman reminded her that she had not yet done her exercises today. She wrinkled her short nose in a whimsical grimace as she crossed to the barre, kicked off her shoes and dutifully commenced on a series of pliés. Since she would never dance professionally, the exercises were rather a waste of time, but their performance had become a kind of ritual. She was even mildly fanciful about them, feeling that somehow they kept her in touch with Maman—that perhaps, if she kept faith with her in this childish fashion, some day she would be rewarded by hearing words of approbation spoken in that dear remembered voice. And in any

case it was something definite to do. The February
day was gloomy with the threat of rain, no weather
for either walking or riding. She wondered if Melly
had finished the letter to Philip that had detained
her in her own room. It must be a long one to keep
her for close on an hour.

She finished with pliés and began on battements.
How must it feel to pour out one's inmost thoughts
on paper, secure in the knowledge that the recipient
would think them of prime importance and read
them with sympathy and even partisan support? She
sighed faintly, envying Melly's secure haven in the
devotion of the faithful Philip, and, on the thought,
the door opened abruptly and Melly came in.

As was only right and proper in one whose duty
was to set a good example, Melly was always me-
ticulously neat. She was twenty-six years old, and
twenty-six years of rigid discipline had left their
mark. Her bearing was sedate, her voice rather flat.
The only display of unbridled emotion that she had
ever permitted herself had been a speaking pressure
of Fleur's hand when she had found words inadequate to express her regret at their approaching
separation.

Judge, then, of Fleur's amazement when this
paragon of propriety positively erupted into the
schoolroom with something of the appearance of a
badly startled hare. Her neatly banded locks were
in unusual disarray, her mild brown eyes so dis-
tended that they seemed about to pop out of their
sockets, and she was pink and breathless. Yet she

seemed at a loss for words and could only stare helplessly at her erstwhile pupil, sinking agitatedly into a chair and blinking myopically at Fleur as if she had never seen her before.

"Goodness!" exclaimed the startled girl. "What in the world has happened to put you all on end, Melly? Is it Grandpapa?"

Miss Melling nodded, gulped, and actually sat for a moment with her mouth open. Such an unprecedented loss of composure was quite frightening.

"Not bad news of Maman?" ventured Fleur anxiously. Miss Melling shook her head.

When her employer had obligingly informed her of the plans that he had made for his granddaughter's future, he had gruffly intimated that he left it to her to tell the wench. "Females are better at such things." he condescended largely. "And you being about to enter parson's mousetrap yourself will make it seem more natural-like."

Even in the nerve-shattered condition consequent upon his startling disclosure she had been flattered by this recognition of her abilities—the first courtesy, indeed, that she had ever received from him. Alas! Mr. Pennington's faith would have been sadly shaken by her present behaviour. Realising that she must say *something,* his emissary gripped the edge of her chair with both hands, drew a deep breath and announced baldly, "I have to tell you, my love, that your grandfather has arranged a very advantageous marriage for you."

It was Fleur's turn to stare open-mouthed, slender

dark brows drawing together, what colour she had fading as she realised that Melly was serious.

"Who?" she breathed tautly.

"Marcus Blayden," said Melly quietly, reverting to her normal staid manner now that the worst was over. She said nothing more for a moment or two, allowing the girl time to adjust herself to the startling news of the sudden change in her immediate prospects. And small wonder that she was startled, even shocked, thought Melly indignantly. Arranged marriages might be perfectly commonplace. There could be no doubting that parents knew best and were well within their rights in arranging them. For her part, Melly, happily betrothed to a young man whom she had known from childhood, thought that this particular arranged match was absolute iniquitous. The contracting parties were not even acquainted, yet would, if Mr. Pennington had his way, become man and wife within a sennight. What hope of happiness could there be for Fleur, young, gauche, unarmoured by the very seclusion of the life she had led, if she were given in marriage to a man of Marcus Blayden's stamp? A man of the world, sophisticated, cold-hearted and contemptuous of lesser folk, his acceptance of the bargain purchased by Pennington gold. Yet duty to her employer demanded that she play her part in the unpleasant business. Besides— what else could the child do, if her grandfather was determined?

"I believe that he is quite a personable young

man," she said temperately. "And there can be no denying that, as his wife, you would have a position of the first consequence. To be sure, his father is only a baron but it is one of the oldest creations. The Blaydens set themselves on a very high form."

"But not so high as to turn up their noses at my grandfather's money," said Fleur bitterly, her colour returning as the shock of Melly's news abated.

"I believe it is true that Lord Blayden has sadly reduced his inheritance by his passion for gaming," admitted Miss Melling soberly. "I do not attempt to deceive you, my dear, and must admit to the belief that sheer financial necessity has persuaded him to consent to such a match for his only son. But that does not necessarily mean that it is a bad one. Mr. Blayden may make a perfectly acceptable husband. At least he is young—not yet thirty, I believe. And not to mince matters, since it is plain that social advancement is your grandfather's sole object in promoting the match, he might have offered you to Lord Blayden himself. Now *that* I could not have supported. A man so much older, and wholly given over to his mania for gaming."

"And even as it stands it's quite *Gothic*," protested Fleur, resentment rising as she considered all the implications. "To expect me to marry a man I've not so much as set eyes on, just to satisfy his passion for rank and title, with no regard for my happiness, or, I daresay, for the character and tastes of the bridegroom to whom he consigns me."

"For all we know to the contrary, Mr. Blayden's

character may be well established," urged Miss Melling dutifully, And then, falling to a note of doubt, "Though I *have* heard——" She broke off in confusion. "But there——I daresay the tales were exaggerated, as they so often are."

"What tales?" demanded Fleur.

"Why——only that he was as wild and reckless a blade as ever was thrown on the Town. And surely that is not to be wondered at when one considers his father's example. Besides, that was several years ago. If he is contemplating matrimony we may believe that he has put the follies of youth behind him. Now that I come to think of it, it is months since Mrs. Fordyce, who was my informant, has so much as mentioned his name. So you may rely upon it that her sister in London cannot have unearthed any recent scandal about him."

Fleur pondered this pronouncement judicially. "Well——I had rather marry a man of spirit and enterprise than a virtuous ninny," she decided. "But I don't wish to be married at all. I've seen nothing of the world except High Barrows and school. I want to travel and have adventures and meet interesting people. And then, when I am quite old—— say nineteen or twenty——I want to choose the kind of husband that *I* like, not have one thrust upon me."

Miss Melling shuddered. She could not imagine where her charge had picked up such revolutionary notions. It must come of being half French. Hurriedly she closed her mind to the impulse of sympathy that stirred her, for to encourage any hope that Fleur might cherish of setting her grandfather at defiance would be mistaken kindness. As well might some naked nestling hope to outmanoeuvre a hungry prowling cat.

"Your Grandpapa has arranged for Mr. Blayden to call upon you this afternoon," she warned. "Whatever your feelings in the matter you will be expected to meet him with all due courtesy. It would be foolish—and would only enrage Mr. Pennington—if you were to decline his offer without even seeing him."

Fleur looked mutinous. "Certainly I will receive him," she said with dignity. "I can scarcely refuse him the common usage of hospitality. But for him to be making me an offer when his feelings are no more engaged than my own is quite absurd. Indeed, it is almost insulting. And so I shall tell him," she ended with spirit.

Miss Melling sighed. In general the child was biddable enough. She was a warm-hearted little creature and sincerely attached to her duenna. But once she took a notion into her head she had a determined obstinacy strongly reminiscent of her paternal grandfather.

"Pray remember, my love, that young ladies in your position do *not* choose their own husbands," she said firmly. "They have neither the wisdom nor the experience to do so. Suitable marriages are *always* arranged for them by parents or guardians who are better able to judge."

Fleur sniffed and put up her chin defiantly. "Me, I have no position," she announced. "I am not a lady of long pedigree. Why should I be bound by these outworn conventions? I'm not even English. I'm half French."

Miss Melling was swift to seize the advantage. "And had you been wholly French, brought up in France," she pointed out, "your marriage would have been arranged for you years ago between the respective parents. No one would have consulted *your* wishes. So you are no worse off."

Fleur looked slightly deflated, but not for long. "In that case I would at least have been betrothed to someone in my own rank of life," she argued. "It would have been a—a business arrangement. A partnership. *That* one could respect. But to be sold to a decadent aristocrat just because my grandfather has antiquated notions about consequence and rank and title is no better than slavery and I will resist it to the death!"

Miss Melling eyed her reprovingly. "You had that out of a book," she accused. "Some cheap and trashy romance. Really, Fleur! How *can* you repeat such fustian? And you know very well that it is nothing of the kind. Though to be sure, your intemperate language makes it abundantly clear that you are by far too young to be married."

Fleur flushed rosy red and bit her lip. The phrases *did* sound false and over-dramatic when spoken aloud. Seeing her taken at fault, Miss Melling hurried on, "I do not need to tell you that you have every cause to be grateful to your Grandpapa and that you should study to please him. I do not urge you to accept the match; only to meet Mr. Blayden with courtesy and to keep an open mind until you have come to know him a little. For I must remind you that if your Grandpapa were to cast you off— and when he is in one of his takings there is no saying *what* he will do—you would be in sad case. How would you earn your bread? You will be the first to admit that you are quite unfitted for a post as a governess. You are too young to have the care and companionship of an invalid and you are quite untrained for anything else. It is no light matter to be cast alone and penniless upon the world. I beg you to consider very carefully before you anger Mr. Pennington beyond the point of forgiveness. He has gone to a great deal of trouble to arrange a splendid match for you, and his heart is set on it."

Fleur was sobered if not convinced. Melly had spoken with an earnestness that at least gave her pause. It was all nonsense, of course, about being cast upon the world. Grandpapa would never do so. And even if he did, there must be dozens of things that she, Fleur, could do, even if she wasn't clever enough to be a governess. But it was true that, in his own way, Grandpapa had been good to her. If meeting the Honourable Marcus Blayden with some show of complaisance would appease him, surely she could bring herself to do *that*.

FOUR

IT HAD seemed simple enough, talking to Melly in the familiar security of the schoolroom, to decide what she would say to her unwanted suitor. In the formal atmosphere of the ladies' parlour it was a very different matter, even though she had Melly's support and Grandpapa had mercifully absented himself from the interview. "The pair of 'em'll manage better without me," he had bluntly informed Miss Melling. "What's more they'd do better without you either. Yes, yes, I *know* she can't receive him unchaperoned. I may not have been born into the world hosed and shod, but I do know that much. You'll have to show your front to play pro-

priety, seeing as the Blaydens are such high stick-
lers, but I still hold to it that a man and a maid'll
deal best left to themselves, and if so be as you can
shab off without giving offence, you do it. Or send
'em out to walk about the grounds, or some such
ploy. You can do *that*, can't you?"

Miss Melling glanced through the library win-
dow at the bleak prospect of lowering sky and rain-
sodden lawns and shivered involuntarily. "Perhaps
the conservatories," she said doubtfully, "though
indeed, at this season of the year there is little to be
seen—"

"And little they'll care for that," snorted her employer. "Just you give 'em a chance to settle the
business with no one by. Them's my *orders*, remember. The chap'll know well enough how to set about
it so long as you're not there to hinder him, and the
sooner it's settled the better I'll be pleased."

So it was that when Marcus was ushered into the
parlour he found only the correctly colourless Miss
Melling and a white-faced frightened-looking child
waiting to greet him. He had come reluctantly,
cursing the weakness that had driven him to submit
to his father's scheming yet unable to devise any
means of crying off without sacrificing his sister. An
earlier interview with Mr. Pennington had been
difficult enough, but at least it had taken place on
his own ground at Blayden and there had been no
need to beat about the bush. The older man had
been bluntly businesslike, setting out his terms for
the proposed settlements with no more emotion

than if he had been selling a bale of goods. Nor were those terms ungenerous, and, if the girl herself was willing, he supposed he might as well agree to the bargain. He had stood out for a week's grace in which he and Miss Pennington might become acquainted. That would at least allow him time to discover whether she was being forced into marriage against her will. Having met her formidable grandfather, such a discovery would not surprise him. And there was certainly nothing in his first sight of her to correct this impression.

She seemed a shy, spiritless little thing, very young and obviously overawed by the circumstances of his visit. Her correct curtsy and the wooden formality of her greeting were evidence only of the submissiveness to which, his father had claimed, she had been trained. Probably the hint of breathlessness in the soft voice and the slight quiver in the cold fingers that rested briefly in his clasp were a more accurate indication of her feelings. He felt again that faint flicker of pity for her helplessness. It was irrational, for no one could force the girl into marriage if she was really unwilling, but she was certainly uncomfortably placed with her juggernaut of a grandfather exerting all his energies to force her consent and only this drab little cypher of a companion to give her womanly guidance in the making of a wise decision. Some shadow of the tenderness that he kept for Deborah caused him to relax a little the cool arrogance of his bearing, softened the bitter set of his mouth. He exerted

himself to coax his prospective bride out of the
paralysing shyness that seemed to have bereft her
of the power of speech. He had considerable social
address and, when he so chose, a pleasant easy
manner that lent warmth and interest to perfectly
commonplace remarks. By the time that they had
dealt faithfully with the vagaries of the weather, the
discomforts of travel at this season of the year and,
on a higher intellectual plane, the deliberations of
the politicians at present assembled in congress in
distant Vienna, Fleur was so far restored to her
normal poise as to be able to take a modest share
of the conversational burden and even to spare part
of her attention for covert study of Mr. Blayden's
appearance.

Her acquaintance with the male sex was limited.
Apart from her grandfather, the vicar of the parish
and the rather ineffectual dancing master at school,
she had a bowing acquaintance with such of the
local gentry and yeomanry as were members of the
hunt. In all her short life she had never met such a
man as Marcus Blayden at close quarters. Save for
his height and his athletic figure, he was not in the
least like any of the dream heroes of her girlish
fancy. In features, air and bearing he bore far too
close a resemblance to his father. She had always
been repelled by Lord Blayden's high-bred air of
cool indifference to the affairs of less exalted folk.
The son had the same cold grey eyes, heavy lidded
beneath level dark brows. His strongly marked
features seemed to indicate a masterful disposition,

and though his voice was deep and pleasant and his present manners conciliating, there was no hint of softness in the lines about his mouth. He would be an ill man to cross, thought Fleur, paying little heed to the remarks that he was addressing to Melly, but, if looks were anything to go by, a staunch ally in time of need. For despite his soft speech and languid bearing there was about him an aura of scarce-contained energy, a power and magnetism that was new and exciting to the inexperienced girl. She sensed it plainly enough but could not be sure whether it attracted or frightened.

A pause in the placid flow of talk roused her from her absorption. Melly was regarding her with a censorious air, while about Mr. Blayden's mouth there hovered for the first time the suggestion of a smile. She coloured guiltily, aware that she had been caught frankly staring at him.

"Mr. Blayden was enquiring if you would care to drive out with him tomorrow to visit his sister," said Melly severely.

"That would be d-delightful," stammered Fleur confusedly. How *could* she have allowed her thoughts to stray so far? "I have seen Miss Blayden in church and have often wished to make her acquaintance."

"She does not go about very much," explained her brother, and went on to speak of Deborah's frail health and of the pleasure that such a visit would give her, privately calculating how much longer he must endure this boring exchange of inanities. Miss

Pennington might be as meek as his father had claimed. It seemed to him that they had knocked all the spirit out of her, if, indeed, she had ever had any.

He was presently able to revise this opinion. Discussion of the arrangements for the proposed drive caused Miss Pennington to say wistfully that she had never driven in anything more exciting than her grandfather's carriage. Did Mr. Blayden drive a curricle or, perhaps, a crane neck phaeton?

Mr. Blayden, admitting to the possession of a curricle, regretted that he had left it in Town when he received his father's summons north, but pointed out that the inclement weather would, in any event, have rendered its use ineligible for the proposed expedition.

He was immediately aware that the careless mention of his father's summons had been a blunder. The eager interest that had so transformed the small pale face vanished and it seemed for a moment that she was about to withdraw once more behind the barrier of punctilious civility. Fortunately a happy reference to the matched chestnuts that he was accustomed to drive in Town was sufficient to distract her. As he spoke of their perfect manners and high spirits and answered eager questions about their age, conformation and breeding, it became apparent that Miss Pennington had vitality and intelligence enough when her interest was fairly caught. She wanted to know what horses he was driving today, but as Lord Blayden had recently reduced his stable he had to confess that they were only hirelings and nothing out of the common. Whereupon she invited him to go with her to the stables to inspect an animal that was, she ventured to think, very *much* out of the common.

Mindful of her employer's instructions, Miss Melling raised no objection to this proposal, merely insisting that her charge should put on a warm pelisse before venturing out of doors. For her own part she proposed to stay snugly by the parlour fire, which she proceeded to do, a little anxious still for Fleur's future, despite a pleasant first impression of Mr. Blayden's personality, but comfortably aware that she had fulfilled her orders to a nicety.

But a stable, however well kept, is scarcely the best setting for exchanges of an intimate nature. Even had he wished to broach the delicate business that had brought him visiting at High Barrows, Mr. Blayden would have been sorely put about to find a suitable opportunity, for in addition to the deep interest in his arrival displayed by Miss Pennington's groom and a couple of stable lads supposedly occupied in cleaning tack, there was Mr. Pennington's coachman, hospitably determined to play host to so distinguished a visitor to his domain, while the girl herself was so absorbed in pointing out the virtues and qualities of the bay mare that her grandfather had just given her for her seventeenth birthday that she seemed quite oblivious of the fact that his visit had been paid with the avowed intent of making her an offer of marriage.

There was an emergent twinkle in Mr. Blayden's cool grey eyes as he said all that was proper in praise of the mare and of several other equine friends who came to snuffle eagerly and hopefully at the girl's hands and whose soft eyes regarded her reproachfully when her pockets were shown to be empty. Mr. Blayden took a firm step in her esteem when a search of *his* pockets produced several grubby-looking sugar lumps. He offered them rather shamefacedly, assuring her that it was not his habit to call on ladies with pockets so furnished, and that if he had brought his own man with him to Blayden he would certainly not have been suffered to do so, but Miss Pennington, accepting the proffered bounty with enthusiasm and sharing it with scrupulous fairness between her several pensioners was clearly disposed to think well of a gentleman who came calling so sensibly equipped for any eventuality.

So powerfully did this small incident work upon her feelings that it was not long before she was chattering away gaily as though she had known him for ever, pouring into an amused and tolerant ear a dozen confidences that, in the absence of a sympathetic listener, had never previously found utterance. The bay mare, he learned, was really called Chérie, though Grandpapa, who detested all things French, not so much from innate patriotism as because the French wars had jeopardised certain business interests, believed the name to be Sherry—"Because of the colour, of course."

"A natural enough assumption," agreed Marcus solemnly, watching the play of light over the mare's rippling hide. And then, tentatively, "Is Mr. Pennington so formidable that such deception is necessary?"

The girl laughed quite naturally. "Why, no! He is, perhaps, a little rigid in his notions. And since his rages are very uncomfortable for anyone within earshot, one does not choose to ruffle him without good cause. But I would not have you think me afraid of him, so good as he is to me."

So she is not being constrained against her wish, thought Marcus, reading far more into the simple remark than the speaker had intended, since she had spoken from instinctive loyalty rather than conviction. In that case, he might as well pursue this rather odd form of courtship. He decided to venture upon a mild compliment.

"For my part," he said lazily, "I cannot assent to his dislike of all things French. The *flowers* of France, for instance, are quite delightful, and mingled with our sturdier stock produce blooms of rare charm."

Her reaction to the careless flattery surprised him. He had half expected so young and inexperienced a damsel to be thrown into confusion—blushing, stammering, protesting. Miss Pennington eyed him with a calm shrewdness strongly reminiscent of her grandsire and favoured him with a tiny unsmiling curtsy. For a moment he wondered if she was so slow-witted that she had not caught the allusion, but her curtsy was clearly intended to acknowledge the compliment. She was not imperceptive—she was just unimpressed. Slightly nettled, for though he held the hyperbole of compliment in tolerant scorn he had thought the play on the girl's name not ill-chosen, he awaited her reply with interest.

"You must not think that I am ashamed of my French blood," said the lady kindly. "It was awkward at school, of course. I disliked being called Froggie. And some of the girls were jealous because I was the show pupil when French speaking was in question. But one grows accustomed and I no longer stand in need of consolation."

The rebuff was unmistakable. The friendly youngster who had talked so eagerly of her horses had withdrawn behind a barrier of cool reserve. In his deeper consciousness Marcus was aware that there must have been a considerable degree of hurt to have left a wound that still could not endure the lightest touch, but at the moment his paramount feeling was annoyance at having laid himself open to such a set-down from a chit scarce out of the schoolroom. Masculine pride demanded that he make a prompt recovery.

"That was scarcely my intention, Miss Pennington," he said smoothly. And then in easy colloquial French, "Though I cannot lay claim to French blood I have a considerable fondness for that lovely land. My mother's sister married a Frenchman and as a child I spent many months in her home in the

Loire country. Childhood attachments die hard. I had hoped, in your society, to revive them."

The words had scarcely left his lips before he regretted them. Why use so weighty a weapon to crush so frail an adversary? And why, above all, admit a stranger, even if she was a prospective bride, so far into his confidence? But it was done, and he must abide the consequences.

The stiff little face broke into such a medley of confused emotions that he realised for the first time how tight a hold the child had kept on them. There was surprise, of course; there was guilt and apology mingled that she should so have mistaken him. But above all there was excitement and delight at hearing her mother's tongue spoken as she had not heard it since that mother's going.

Words bubbled from her eager lips in tumultuous disorder. "I did not know—pray forgive me—I thought it was just a silly compliment. You will think me conceited beyond belief—I should have guessed you would not stoop to such foolish nonsense. And you have been in France and know and love it as Maman did. Oh! You cannot imagine how wonderful it is to hear you speak her language as she did. But yet! You *do* know. It is as you have said—that childhood fondness dies hard."

She, too, had lapsed into the dear familiar tongue, mobile lips and fluttering hands betraying her French ancestry in a gay abandonment of the sober way of speech and gesture in which she had been

so carefully drilled. They strolled back to the house.
Shaken completely out of her shyness and distrust,
she was her natural self. He found her warmhearted,
generous and comical by turns. His good opinion of
her grew and he found himself pitying the loneliness
that made her catch so eagerly at congenial companionship. His father had chosen better than he
had dreamed. There would be no hardship in taking
to wife this ardent clear-minded child. It did not
occur to him that his attitude was that of a kindly
elder brother; that he had never even considered her
as a woman but rather as an appealing and faintly
pathetic waif whom he was willing to take under
his protection.

Very different was Miss Pennington's reaction.
She had summoned all her forces to meet and reject
an unwanted suitor. Instead she had found a veritable Prince Charming. Impressed at the outset by
Mr. Blayden's dark distinction, lulled by his easy
courtesy and delighted when he showed an understanding of horseflesh that outmatched her own,
his easy use of her mother tongue and his obvious
affection for the French way of life proved a
clincher. Without hesitation she tumbled head over
heels in love with him. Rapturously would she entrust her life into those strong slender hands, whose
casual touch, as they automatically proffered the
courtesies due to a lady, sent such exquisite sensa-
tions thrilling through her responsive young body.

Nor did it occur to the lady, in her innocence and

inexperience, that almost any personable young man who chose to single her out for particular attention might well appear in an unduly favourable light.

FIVE

MARCUS'S stipulated week passed swiftly. Perhaps it could not truthfully be said that he furthered his acquaintance with his promised wife—for the marriage was now agreed—but at least they spent as much time in each other's society as convention permitted, and succeeded in spending it quite pleasantly. The weather favoured them. Three days of warm sunshine swelled the willow buds, brought out thousands of aconites and snowdrops in the park at Blayden, and encouraged the betrothed pair to ride together daily and even, on one occasion, to persuade Deborah to accompany them in a gentle amble over the soft turf. Fleur was quietly but

ecstatically happy; Marcus comfortably resigned.
The wedding day was fixed, and though February
was a sad month for such a function and the notice
almost indecently short, Mr. Pennington did not
despair of seeing his reception rooms well filled. The
very haste of the arrangements and the fact that his
grand-daughter was marrying the heir of Blayden
would titillate the curiosity of the local gentry. It
was generally known that High Barrows offered its
guests every conceivable luxury—such dishes as
must tempt the most jaded palate and wines of the
very finest vintage. Yes. They would come. They
might raise their eyebrows and whisper and smile
behind their fans. But they would come.

Only Miss Melling had reservations as to the
nature of the marriage that was to follow—for a
wedding is one thing, a marriage quite another. To
her quiet good sense this one seemed a very
unequal business. Because her love was so new-
sprung and strange, Fleur cradled it close in her
heart. Her manner towards her betrothed was pleasantly undemonstrative so that no one else appeared
to realise that she had given all her young adoration to the attractive stranger upon whom her
grandfather had chosen to bestow her hand. But
Melly knew. And Melly deeply deplored the fervour that glowed in the great grey eyes when they
rested on her idol. The child was bemused, as helpless in the grip of first love as any sacrificial lamb.
Mr. Pennington saw only the prompt submission
to his will—and plumed himself upon his excellent

management. Lord Blayden permitted himself the
faintest sigh of gratification that his difficulties were
in a fair way of being settled. Only Melly foresaw
the tragedy that might lie ahead if Mr. Blayden
proved unworthy. But since she could do nothing
to prevent the marriage she kept her doubts and
fears to herself and devoted her energies to the practical problems that must be solved if all the arrangements were to meet with Mr. Pennington's exacting
demands. The marriage was being pushed on with
insensate haste, thought Melly indignantly. Did he
fear that one or other of the contracting parties
might yet cry off? And went off to oversee the
sewing maids who were working frantically on
Fleur's wedding gown.

Still the mild weather held. Pale February sunshine blessed the pale little bride who went timor-
ously but hopefully to her wedding in the quiet
village church. Lord Blayden had urged the use of
the private chapel at Blayden for the ceremony, but
private chapels were one appurtenance of the aris-
tocracy that Mr. Pennington did not approve. As
became his standing in the neighbourhood, he was
a professed member of the established church but
he came of sturdy nonconformist stock and private
chapels, to him, smacked of popery. The marriage
would take place in the parish church and everyone
should see that all was open and above board and
nothing havey-cavey. Lord Blayden, who had hoped
to avoid such public association with one whom he
privately designated as a money-grubbing cit, was

forced to accede. Time enough to take a stronger stand when the knot was duly tied.

The events of her wedding day never seemed quite real to Fleur. Even her mirror showed her a stranger. That was not Fleur Pennington—that tall slender creature clad in white silk and muffled in a hooded cloak of white velvet. The swansdown that lined and edged the cloak lay like frozen snowflakes against the darkness of her hair. She might be the ice maiden of Maman's fairy tales rather than a warm and living girl.

Melly, hovering anxiously about her, re-arranged the hood and put a posy of snowdrops into her hands. The child looked pale and overwrought. Melly was not much given to romantic metaphor. Perhaps it was the emotion aroused by a wedding that caused her to liken her charge to a windflower, a plant that flourished best in quiet secluded places, delicate and pure. Devoutly she prayed that the girl might also have the resilience, the powers of endurance of that seemingly fragile flower. She stooped and dropped a light kiss on the pale cheek.

"I must go now. Your grandfather is waiting for you in the library. You have ten minutes before you need set out," she said, and whisked herself out of the room to make last-minute adjustments to her own toilet before hurrying to take her place in church.

Grandpapa, too, seemed almost a stranger. He had chosen to dignify the occasion by arraying himself in knee breeches, silk stockings and richly laced brocade coat, announcing that he knew just as well as the next one what the real swells wore. What was good enough for the queen's court would be just the thing for his grand-daughter's wedding. The costume did nothing to enhance a stocky figure with a tendency to corpulence. But even more startling than his attire was his unexpected display of softer feelings.

Fleur knew that just at present she stood high in his good graces on account of what he took to be her obedience to his wishes. But when he clumsily produced a box which held a very fine pearl necklet and proceeded to fasten the pretty gaud about her throat, fumbling with the catch and patting her cheek with a grunted, "You're a good little puss after all," she was taken quite by surprise. When he further added, "And don't fear he'll not do right by you, for it's me that holds the purse strings and I'll see to it that my fine gentleman treats you just as he ought. A position of first consequence in the county is what you'll have. Presented at court, too, I shouldn't wonder," she found this hint of compunction surprisingly touching.

Mr. Pennington hesitated momentarily. Women were kittle cattle; especially young 'uns. Still, the girl had no mother to tell her what was expected of her in return for these promised splendours. "And see *you* do *your* duty," he warned bluntly. "An heir for Blayden is what they'll be wanting. And it's what I want, too. So no prudish shrinkings from your lawful wedded spouse. Obedience and submission are a wife's first duties."

Maidenly shrinkings had been far from Fleur's mind, but at this harsh grasp on the diaphanous fabric of her dreams she did indeed shrink, colour staining her pale cheeks as she whispered meekly, "Yes, Grandpapa."

He rubbed his hands together in satisfaction at the prospect in contemplation. "My great grandson, Lord Blayden," he said, half to himself. And then, more briskly, "Well, maybe I'll not be above ground to see the day, but that's what he'll be. My blood in his veins. And my brains in his noodle I do hope and trust, so's he'll make a better job of being a lordship than your new papa-in-law has done. Bringing an abbey to a grange in his own lifetime and all on the fall of a card or the dice! Young Robert'll have more sense in *his* cockloft—for you'll name him for me, of course."

Further confidences on the subject of that paragon who should some day be the eleventh Baron Blayden were prevented by the footman's announcement that the carriage was waiting to take them to church.

It is not, in the general way, the grandfather of the bride who dominates the scene at a wedding, but *this* wedding marked the achievement of the ambition that had driven Robert Pennington for more than half a lifetime. Frustrated in his plans for his only son, that ambition had been held in check for fifteen years. Released now, reborn in the light of the marriage that he had achieved for Alexander's daughter, it soared to new heights. Who was to say that his great-grandson would be content with a mere barony? The lad might take a fancy to being an earl or a marquis, and with Pennington acumen to plot his course and Pennington gold behind him, who was to say that something of the sort might not be contrived? It was the manifest duty of the present Robert Pennington, the founder of the family fortunes, the architect of its greatness, to see to it that his descendent should have ample resources to draw upon.

His rubicund countenance wreathed, for once, in smiles, his brain busily weaving its plans for the future, he bustled about among his guests with energetic goodwill, happily unaware of the amusement that he was causing. Lord Blayden was not a popular figure. His cold reserve, the infrequency and brevity of his visits to Blayden, and his known indifference to the welfare of a young daughter who was held in affection by many of those present, had not served to endear him to his neighbours. There were covert smiles and shaking shoulders as Mr. Pennington approached him with cheerful *bon-homie*, slapped him heartily on the back, dug a plebian elbow into his aristocratic ribs and assured him jovially that, between them, they had done a good day's work and now it was up to the young couple to show what *they* could do.

Marcus saw his wife blush vividly at her grandfather's crudity and marked with approval that she neither drooped a shamed head nor even put up a

hand to shield her face from observation. Instead
she held herself erect and still for a moment, as
though testing her self control, and then turned to
speak quietly to the Vicar's wife who chanced to be
standing beside her.

For his own part he was growing heartily bored
with the festivities and wished them safely over.
Country functions always tended to drag on endlessly, especially at this season of the year when
people who had not met since snow and thaw had
made the roads impassable were eager to catch up
on news of families and friends. Their interest in
the bridal pair temporarily satisfied, they were
settling down contentedly to discussion of their own
affairs. It would be another hour, he judged, before
he and Fleur could reasonably break up the party.
A pity that they were only going to Blayden. If he
had decided to take his wife to France for the
honeymoon—a notion that he had toyed with briefly
and then rejected—they could have pleaded the
necessities of travel as an excuse for early departure.
But though the Bourbon was comfortably established on his throne and the man who had sub-
jugated most of Europe was now exercising a
restricted dominion over the tiny island of Elba,
France was still suffering from the ravages of war.
It would take years to restore the countryside to the
lush beauty of his childhood memory. Too many
lads who should have been tilling the soil had been
called to the colours. The Emperor's armies had
good cause for pride in their achievements but they

had drained their country's life blood to exhaustion point. The France of today was no place for a honeymoon.

Nor was Marcus himself in honeymoon mood. His bride was a nice child. He was growing quite attached to her. Their marriage would develop into an amicable arrangement where each of them would contentedly go their separate ways. If, thanks to her grandfather's wealth, Blayden should be preserved to him, he would expect her to give him an heir to the property, but he would ask no more of her than that. Meanwhile he guessed she would be grateful for respite. He had no intention of claiming his marital rights though this could scarcely be accounted as forbearance since he had no particular desire to do so. Let the child grow up. Then they would see.

It was already dusk when they set out for Blayden, and since the four of them travelled together in Lord Blayden's coach there was no opportunity for conversation of an intimate nature between husband and wife. Fleur had very little notion as to the pattern of her future life. She knew that they were to spend several weeks at Blayden, but after that it was not clear whether they would spend most of their time in London or at the Cobham manor. Marcus had once said that his London lodging was very small—a mere bachelor *pied-à-terre*—and quite unsuited for a married pair, so presumably they would have to hire or buy a

larger house. At the moment she was not looking
so far ahead.

Dinner was a silent meal. His Lordship kept
Town hours, even at Blayden, but though it was
past seven o'clock before they sat down to table,
no one was hungry. Either the lavish assortment of
epicurean delicacies that had been spread before
them at the wedding breakfast had dulled their
appetites, or the gloomy chill of the vast dining-
room at Blayden was sufficient to damp the spirits
of so small a party. Deborah had excused herself
and retired early to her own apartments, pleading
fatigue after the day's excitement. Lord Blayden
scarcely spoke except to enquire Fleur's preference
between the several dishes that were set before him.
Marcus did his best to maintain an easy flow of
small talk. Conversation with various of the wedding
guests had assured him that the roads to the north
were reasonably clear. Would Fleur enjoy an expedition to Carlislc? The Cathedral and the Castle
were considered very fine if she cared for antiquities,
and there were some good shops. They had married
in such haste that there had been no time to choose
a wedding gift for her. They could look about them
for some suitable token. Unless, of course, she preferred to wait until they went to London, where
there would be a much wider choice. Fleur, who
desired neither entertainment nor gifts, but only
to be left alone with her husband and held close
in the safe shelter of his arms, feigned polite en-

thusiasm and said all that was proper in a primly correct little voice.

Mention of the Metropolis, however, evoked some response from Lord Blayden, who emerged from his abstraction to announce that *he* would be leaving for Town next day, and that as he proposed to set out betimes in order to make the most of the hours of daylight, he would bid them farewell now. Since, moreover, he had several estate matters to put in hand before his departure, they must forgive him if he now withdrew to the estate office where his steward was already awaiting him. No doubt, he added, a faintly bored curl to his thin lips, they would contrive to amuse themselves very well without his society.

His son's adieux were curt since he was hard put to it to swallow his anger at his father's cavalier treatment of his new daughter-in-law. He could only hope that the unpleasant implication in the final remark had passed over her innocent head. Had he felt any desire for an immediate consummation of his marriage, that remark would have killed it. It was worse than Mr. Pennington's sly jests, since they stemmed from ignorance and were, at least, dictated by good will.

"My father is not much addicted to the wine cup," he apologised brusquely, anger still riding him. "Very rarely does he linger over it unless we are entertaining guests of a different way of thinking. And since I do not care to drink alone, will you permit me to escort you to the drawing-room?"

The next two hours seemed endless, though he exerted himself to the utmost to entertain her, telling her the histories of the many strange objects accumulated by his ancestors over the years and now relegated to decorative purposes, inviting her to try out the tones of the harpsichord—an invitation promptly and shudderingly declined—and at last, in desperation, suggesting that they play cards. The atmosphere improved a little when he began teaching her to play picquet. The need to concentrate on the fall of the cards and on the assessment of her chances proved a better distraction than mere conversation. By the time that the tea tray was brought in he could congratulate himself on a certain degree of success. She was talking more naturally, even smiling occasionally, and once, when she defeated him handsomely by retaining an unexpected guard to the spade king, she actually chuckled. Had he been thinking only of the game he would have said that, having inherited a good deal of her grandfather's shrewdness, she would some day make a very fair player.

But these signs of relaxation vanished with the arrival of the tea tray. She poured out for him competently enough, but she fell silent again. He could only suppose her to be terrified of the initiation into the mysteries of the marriage bed that she must suppose to be imminent. It was a deuced awkward business but somehow he must set her fears at rest.

He put his cup back on the tray. "You must be

very tired, my dear," he said gently. "May I suggest that you retire as soon as you have drunk your tea? Betty will see that you have all you need—which reminds me that we must see about finding a suitable maid for you." His voice deepened a little. "You need not fear that your rest will be disturbed. I know that I am still all but a stranger. The demands of our families have brought us together in marriage but I claim no rights as your husband. Let us learn to know each other, become friends—as I think we have already begun to do. For the present that is sufficient."

He stooped and kissed her hand, then, after a brief hesitation, her cheek, and left her to the tea tray and her lonely grandeur.

When Betty had disrobed her and seen that the bed was well warmed and the windows fast shut against any breath of treacherous night air, the new Mrs. Blayden cried herself to sleep.

SIX

BUT she was very tired. Sleep came quickly, and youth and good health set a brighter aspect on the morning. Sunshine, brilliant if fickle, beckoned to an inspection of her new home and the knowledge that her intimidating father-in-law was, by this time, well on his way to London, made the prospect an inviting one. And finally, if her husband was not in love with her, he was at least kind and considerate. Fleur was young and romantic, but there was a very practical side to her nature, deriving as much from her French blood as from the mercantile strain. Her husband had left her lonely but inviolate. Better so than that he should have possessed her in careless lust just because she was his chattel. Perhaps, after all, his way was best. They were bound together indissolubly. There was time enough for love to grow, so that their eventual mating might be as blissful as her dreams.

And indeed, as the days passed, it seemed as though events were moving gently but steadily towards this desirable outcome. Gradually the awkwardness born of unfamiliarity and tension began to diminish. There was so much to see and to do that the hours passed all too swiftly. That projected expedition to Carlisle never materialised. On the brink of departure Lord Blayden had casually informed his son that he might give orders for the redecoration and refurbishing of the apartments in the west wing that would, in future, be set aside for the occupation of the young couple whenever they chose to visit Blayden, so even when the unseasonably mild weather gave way to the gales and squally rainstorms of March, there was still ample food for discussion during the long hours spent beside the library fire or strolling about the big shabby rooms that were to be transformed. Since Deborah, whose health appeared to have benefited considerably from her father's departure, spent much of her time in their company there was no sense of constraint to inhibit the comfortable companionship that strengthened with every shared plan and pleasure. Only when they bade each other goodnight and Fleur accepted the grave kiss upon her cheek which had become the accepted formula of parting did she sometimes wonder wistfully how long it would be before her husband crossed the impalpable barrier that kept them apart.

In fact, neither of them realised how much closer they had drawn to each other; how well propinquity had done its subtle work. In the easy association granted by Deborah's continual presence, the rigidly correct mould into which Fleur had been schooled rapidly disintegrated. Within a week she was saying exactly what came into her head. And what came into her head, though usually sensible, was frequently impudent and occasionally quite shocking to the tradition-bound Blaydens. She thought the housekeeping arrangements at Blayden antiquated beyond belief and had no hesitation in saying so. Who, *par exemple*—the conversation generally dropped into French when she was most moved, and ended with apologies to Deborah, who was less fluent than her brother—invented the archaic rule that none of the maids must be seen in the reception rooms after eight o'clock in the morning? The result was simply that the work was scamped by chilled sleepy girls who had been roused at five and would have worked all the better for another hour in their beds. The library and the breakfast-room, yes. That was reasonable. But the other rooms were never used before noon, so— why? And her fascinated audience listened and were compelled to assent, though since it was not for *them* to order the domestic arrangements of Lord

Blayden's household there was nothing that they could do about it.

Somewhere among these impulsive outbursts, the story of the regular practising at the barre emerged. Why not? One should not be ashamed of one's blood and breeding. One was, after all, what one was.

The confidence was given first in an idle moment to Deborah, who listened absorbedly to the exposition of an art that must for ever be closed to her.

"Though I could play for you," she suggested tentatively. "I am thought to have a reasonable aptitude for music. Perhaps, now," she added, innocent of any hurtful intent, "Papa will be able to buy me one of the new pianofortes that I have wanted for so long."

The upshot of this conversation was made visible some days later when Deborah invited her new sister to come and look at the old nursery suite adjacent to her own apartments. For in the day nursery, previously swept bare of all but the old brass fireguard, a very dilapidated rocking horse and a low, comfortable nursing chair, was now installed a new, shiny pianoforte, while a barre ran the length of one wall.

Fleur gasped and exclaimed and hugged Deborah excitedly, all the time protesting that she should not have done it.

"But I didn't," said Deborah, surprised. "How could I? It was Marc who managed it all—and so quickly, too. He said it was a queer sort of a marriage gift, but if that was what you wanted you should have it."

Marcus, when he arrived to inspect the result of his providing, went a little further than this. Since Deborah was present it was safe to tease his wife a little, an impulse which he found assailing him with growing frequency. He surveyed the new set-up with solemnity, insisted that Deb should try the tone of the new instrument and then said seriously, "It's all very well. I can see that we have made ample provision for our daughters. A whole corps de ballet may use that barre. But what of our sons? One broken-down charger! Touched in the wind, too, if I mistake not." He made a careful inspection of the rocking horse, still fiery-eyed and scarlet of nostril but sadly deficient as to mane and tail, and turned to Fleur with an air of deep reproach. "You will have to do better than this, my love," he chided her. And then took pity on her crimson confusion and enquired sensibly whether the barre was at the right height, the floor surface suitable, in fact, did she like his gift?

Between thankfulness that he had stopped teasing and delight in his thought for her she forgot to be shy and ran to fling her arms about him and, for the first time, voluntarily kissed his cheek. "It's quite the nicest thing you could have given me," she assured him warmly. "You were a darling to think of it. *Two* darlings," she added conscientiously, for there could be no doubting that the impetus came from Deb.

But she would not have him watch her when she practised, however cunningly he pleaded. Even when he resorted to blackmail, asking plaintively how he could be sure that she really liked his gift unless he saw it in use, she stood firm. Finally he said, "And your wifely submission, sweetheart? If I remember aright, you promised to obey me."

That was unfair, as he very well knew, since it was unanswerable. And on this occasion, as it chanced, they were alone. The grey eyes that had learned to meet his own so frankly were lowered in swift confusion and vivid colour mantled in the creamy skin. Marcus surprised himself by saying softly, "And very soon, my sweet, I mean to remind you more fully of those promises that you made. We know each other better, now, do we not?"

He would have drawn her into his arms and kissed her. Indeed he found himself extremely desirous of doing so. But at that moment Deborah came in and the opportunity was gone.

Nevertheless the small incident stirred him to awareness of the change in his attitude towards his wife. He was scarcely, he supposed, in love with her in the high romantic style. That sort of thing was not at all in his line. But she was a taking little thing, young and fresh and vital. And she was his. Moreover those soft red lips, with the delicious arch in the upper one, gave promise of an ardent temperament. The prospect of initiating her into the delights of love was increasingly attractive.

Several times during the remainder of the day Fleur caught him quietly watching her. There was a new quality in his glance. Speculative? Possessive? She could not be sure. But it made her heart beat faster in mingled apprehension and excitement, for there could be no misunderstanding the tenor of his remarks just before Deborah had interrupted them. Perhaps—tonight? An odd little shiver ran over her and the fingers that were turning over the patterns of upholstery materials grew suddenly clumsy. She looked up, only to meet his eyes again. Their glance dropped to her mouth. "That velvet is the very colour of your lips," he said conversationally, and smiled at her. He might just as well have kissed her. She blushed and lowered her gaze and the patterns tumbled to the floor in confusion.

And now, because it seemed that the moment she had so eagerly desired was almost at hand, she wished, with feminine perversity, to hold it off for a little. The present was deliciously exciting, a delicate tip-toe excitement which she knew instinctively could never come again. Once her surrender was made those grey eyes would no longer tease—challenge—invite. And though she might indeed find heaven in his arms, these last few hours of freedom were tantalisingly sweet. They were married—yes. But that was no reason why she should be taken for granted. She wanted to be wooed and won.

It was in this mood that she went up to dress for dinner and looked with disfavour at the simple muslin gown that Betty had laid out for her. She had been married in such haste that there had been no time to think of anything but her wedding gown. All the other dresses that she possessed were the *jeune fille* muslins and jaconets that Melly had chosen for her when she left school. They were charming, but they were quite out of tune with her present tempestuous mood. And neither would she wear her wedding dress, since that would certainly be construed as blatant invitation to the conqueror to claim possession of his prize.

It was then that she remembered the mulberry brocade. She did not know quite what whim had caused her to bring it with her to Blayden, save that she had known and loved it all her life. It was the one treasure that Maman had brought with her on that hurried flight from France, and a foolish thing to have brought, so poor as they were, for it was quite impractical. It was by far too grand for ordinary use as well as being very old fashioned, since it had belonged to Grand'mére. Maman, like Fleur, had always loved it. In her poverty-stricken days she had sometimes been tempted to cut up the glowing breadths into something that might supplement her shabby wardrobe, but her heart had always failed her when the scissors were in her hand. So the dress had survived to lend its glamour to Fleur's childhood.

She could well remember the first time that Maman had permitted her to dress up in it. She had been nine, tall for her age but skinny—as Grandpapa kindly phrased it. The fabric of the gown had fascinated her. In some lights it looked almost black, in others a deep rich crimson. The low-cut bodice with its tiny waist had hung loosely on her slight frame while the skirt lay in folds about her ankles, but the child had seen only the glow and sheen of the heavy silk, and the enraptured face that looked back at her from the mirror had caused Maman to warn soberly of the dangers of vanity. As for the dress, said Maman, it might serve some day for a masquerade. And, forgetting all about the dangers of vanity, she had proceeded to show Fleur just how the hair should be dressed—very simply, high on top of the head and bound with a riband; then secured at the nape of the neck with a flat bow and coaxed to fall over the left shoulder in one shining rolling curl that accentuated the creamy skin exposed by the deep decolletage.

The dress was utterly and completely unsuitable for a family dinner party—and Fleur was utterly and completely determined to wear it. Only last Christmas she had tried it on, one idle afternoon, and she knew that it fitted her perfectly. Had recognised, too, that it transformed her from thin, commonplace little Fleur Pennington into a veritable figure of romance. It was the kind of dress that made one think of secret assignations, elopements, duels and all the trappings of the fabled past. Never mind if Marcus and Deb and the servants thought she had run mad. Tonight she would wear Grand'-mére's dress. And from it draw the courage to face the encounter with her husband that she knew to be imminent.

She set the bell pealing for Betty and hunted through a drawer for the silver ribbon that had been tied around her bridal posy. It would have to do for her hair since she had nothing that matched the muted crimson of the dress. She would wear the silver slippers that she had worn for her wedding and several ruffled petticoats to hold out the full skirts.

Fortunately, Betty was young enough to be infected by her mistress's impetuous behaviour. Never a word of surprise or protest did she utter but devoted all her skill to producing an effect that startled both of them when the unusual toilet was completed. Betty, quite frankly, drew in her breath with an audible hiss. Fleur, already aware of the transformation that the dress could achieve for a plain child, had not allowed for the added effect of the appropriate hair style, to which her shining dark locks were admirably suited. Nor, though this she did not recognise, for the magical glow that love had set about her. She only knew that never had her eyes looked so large and luminous, her lashes so long and silky, her skin so creamy smooth. Indeed this last was a positive embarrassment. Accustomed as she was to modern standards, the low-cut, tight-laced bodice of fifty years ago seemed almost indecent. She tugged anxiously at the heavy curl that hung over her shoulder, trying to loosen it so that it should fall a little lower and veil the curve of her breast.

"They was used to wear fronts of lace and ribbons in them dresses," volunteered Betty suddenly, forgetting her carefully learned genteel accent and reverting to her natural rustic speech in her excitement. "But 'twere only to keep the cold off their chests, not to cover themselves up. So Mum said. And she were maid to old Lady Blayden—'is lordship's Mama. You look proper nice, ma'am. You do so." Recollecting herself, she coughed to cover her lapse and said woodenly. "Will there be anything else, ma'am?" And, on Fleur's shaking her head, hastened to the servants' hall where she regaled the senior members of the hierarchy with the tale of the strange goings on to which she had just been privy.

Fleur went downstairs carefully, holding up skirts that were a good two inches longer than those to which she was accustomed. The Tompion clock at the turn of the stair informed her that she was a little early. The bolting eyes of the unfortunate footman whom she encountered in the hall assured her that her appearance was, at any rate, arresting. The poor man looked for a moment as though he had taken her for a ghost.

Since Lord Blayden's departure the three of them had formed the habit of dining cosily in front of the library fire. Fleur opened the library door, still smiling over her encounter with the footman, and went in.

SEVEN

DEB was not yet down. Marcus was sprawled in leisurely comfort in a chair before the fire, one foot in its elegant evening pump elevated against the ancient stonework of the chimney-piece that framed the glowing logs. His mind had been pleasantly occupied in plans for his immediate future. He could not linger on at Blayden indefinitely. He was needed at Dakers. The busiest season of the year was almost upon them. It was high time that he was back in the saddle. But first he must reach a proper understanding with his wife. He had, he considered, been patient for quite long enough, entirely forgetting that, in the first instance, he had

felt no *im*-patience. The child had been granted all
these weeks to accustom herself to the thought of
wifehood. Now it was time to be done with shilly-
shallying.

He foresaw no particular difficulty. Quite a self-
assured young man, Mr. Marcus Blayden, who,
until his father had brought a comfortable inheritance to ruin, had been a popular target for the
match-making mamas. He had flirted gaily with the
prettiest of the débutantes and had successfully
eluded capture. His dealings with a different class of
female had been, for two or three seasons, the talk
of the Town. To be sure he seemed to have put
aside these youthful follies when he had inherited
his uncle's estate, but rumour still clung about him.
He was reported to have a ravishing mistress tucked
away down in Kent, though heaven knew how he
managed to support such a luxury on a beggar's
pittance. Another version of the tale credited him
with having so deeply attached a married lady of
quality that she had abandoned husband and home
in order to follow her lover into rustic exile. The
knowing ones agreed that there was undoubtedly
some truth in these tales. How else could one
account for the fellow's peculiar comings and
goings? Friends who sought him out at his London
lodging would be told that he was in Kent. Yet if
they were sufficiently persistent to follow him
thither, he was nowhere to be found, while the servants on the Cobham manor were dull oafs who
were wholly absorbed in the processes of agricul-

ture and knew nothing of the master's cantrips. Or perhaps Blayden had trained them to secrecy. If a lady's honour was in question, what else could her protector do?

It was amply plain that the Honourable Marcus had never had cause to doubt his success with the fair sex. Nor did he do so now. A child out of the schoolroom who had never mixed in society and who was already drawn to him? His knowledgeable eye had not missed the fugitive glances, the rising colour, the unsteady fingers. A few compliments, a kiss or two, and she would tumble into his arms. They might dally very pleasantly at Blayden for perhaps another week of honeymoon, but after that he must really make a move.

At least he would not leave the little creature behind, as his father had suggested. She would be happier at Dakers, where she could play at house-keeping on a smaller scale and make the mistakes of inexperience without fear of ridicule. It did not occur to him that he had decided to take her with him simply because he was loath to leave her. In this, at least, he was perfectly sincere. He only wished that he might carry off Deborah as well. Per-haps, now that he was a married man, his father might be brought to consent to Deb's living with them. But that was for the future.

This was the rather self-satisfied gentleman who, lolling idly in front of his library fire, turned his head at the gentle sound of the opening door and came automatically to his feet before he fully appreciated the vision that stood on the threshold.

For a moment the power of speech was reft from him. It was forgiveable. In that moment Fleur was lovely as possibly she might never appear again. The gaiety of her smile over the footman still curved her lips. The knowledge that she looked better than her best kept her head high. Yet there was a half-enquiring, mischievous tilt to that proudly held head that made her vivid little face wholly enchanting. Only the childishly slender arms betrayed the fact that she was not yet fully grown to womanhood.

And in that brief, dazed moment, Marcus caught his first glimpse of the woman she might become. "And I thought her less than pretty!" he remembered in self-scorn. "She is lovely. Radiant. Exquisite."

He never gave a thought to the peculiarity of her costume or her possible reason for choosing it. To him, in that moment of revelation, it was exactly what he would have chosen for her. She was a queen, aware and proud. And a queen can do no wrong.

But only for an instant did complete surprise hold him immobile. Something of his customary poise was recovered as he came to greet her.

"My lady," he said, very formally, and swept her a magnificent bow. Then, on a deeper, more intimate note, "My very lovely sovereign lady."

The last vestige of Fleur's hesitancy fled. He was neither displeased nor mocking. Rather he had slipped into a matching rôle and was playing his part beautifully. He *liked* her. She dimpled delightfully and extended a slim hand for his kiss with right regal grace. Only when he followed up that courtesy by catching her in his arms and kissing her, for the first time, full on the lips, did she show any hint of shyness. Then, indeed, she did resist for a moment, straining away from him against that strong encircling arm. But when his free hand tilted her chin she yielded meekly enough.

Her lips were soft and untaught and very trusting. He made love to her gently, dropping light kisses on cheek and brow and smoothing the lids over the huge solemn eyes with a kiss apiece before he came again to her lips. He felt the shiver that shook the slender body and smiled a little at her innocent response to his practised love-making. But his own emotions were not untouched. The creamy skin smelt deliciously of some subtle perfume. He found her quite intoxicating. And unfortunately this was not the time for further advances in his skillful wooing, since at any moment Deborah would be joining them. He had best resist the temptation to set his lips to the delicate little hollow at the base of the slim throat where he could plainly see the fluttering pulse-beat. He put her from him reluctantly and resumed his rôle as courtier.

"If my lady is pleased to consent, we shall make tonight a special occasion," he suggested, smiling down at her in most disturbing fashion under those sleepy lids. She blushed hotly, reading into the remark a meaning that he had not actually intended, and said, rather breathlessly, "Yes, sir, if it please you."

He guessed her thought but maintained his rôle, bowing slightly as he said, "Then tonight we shall drink the finest wine of France to pledge our life together."

She looked a little puzzled, for, truth to tell, she was little acquainted with wine of any kind.

"Champagne," he exclaimed. "Cool, sparkling, palest gold. You will like it, I promise."

Fleur was doubtful. She watched him ring for Reeves and give the order and as the butler went out said a little anxiously, "Is it an *intoxicating* drink? It would be very shocking if I became drunk."

He chuckled. "Trust me to guard against that! Yes. It *is* an intoxicating drink. You must never drink it save when I am at hand to keep an eye on you. But one glass, or even two, will do no harm, and no other wine is worthy of your dress. It, too, is French, if I mistake not. And has a history?"

Deborah coming in at this point and exclaiming delightedly at Fleur's appearance, the story of the dress was rehearsed in detail and its magnificence duly admired. Dinner—a much simpler meal than Lord Blayden would have countenanced—was gaily informal, with a very French flavour. Fleur told how Grand'mère had worn the mulberry brocade at a ball from which she had presently eloped with the extremely ineligible suitor on whom she had set her heart. Oh, yes! Grand'mère came of good family, but poverty poor, you understand. After her reckless marriage her relatives had completely cast her off so the ball dress was the sole relic of her former standing. But she and Grand-père had been very happy despite their poverty, so Maman had said.

The champagne was opened and drunk and the talk went merrily, Marcus telling now of the time when he had been lost during one of those visits to his aunt's château. He had stolen out one evening on a forbidden fishing trip and grown so absorbed in his sport that he had not noticed the lateness of the hour or the distance that he had wandered along the river bank. A sharp thunderstorm caused him to seek shelter in a chance-found cave, and by the time the downpour eased it was full dark. It seemed to him prudent to stay where he was until daybreak showed him his whereabouts and he settled down to make the best of his bleak quarters, falling asleep almost at once despite their Spartan nature.

His slumbers were, however, rudely interrupted by the arrival of the regular occupant of the cave, a sturdy peasant who, having fallen foul of the authorities over a little matter of taxes, was lying up in the woods until such time as his relatives could scrape up a sum sufficient to ship him off to America, where his independent notions might be better received. This gentleman, who had been making the evening round of his rabbit snares, was somewhat incensed at finding his uninvited guest, particularly as he did so by falling over him and catching his elbow a nasty crack on one of the boulders with which the entrance to the cave was amply furnished. Between the man's rough patois and his savage appearance—for when eventually he kindled a torch, all that could be seen of him was a pair of wildly glittering eyes and a craggy prow of a nose emerging from a matted tangle of hair and beard—Marcus had been convinced that he had fallen into the hands of some brigand chief.

The Marcus of today paused to sip his wine and grin at the fascinated horror in the faces of his two auditors.

"What did he do?" begged Fleur anxiously, her eyes dark with imagined terrors, even though the story-teller sat there before her eyes in very obvious good health.

"Why! He turned out to be a very good sort of fellow. When he saw that I was only a lad, and a fisherman to boot, he shared his supper with me. I was devilish sharp-set by then, having eaten nothing since *déjeuner*. Don't remember that I ever tasted a hunter's stew the equal of that one. I daresay some of my uncle's partridges had gone into it as well as the conies that he admitted to, but I'd no quarrel with that. I left him my catch in fair payment. He said fish'd make a tasty change, since he daren't haunt the river bank in daylight and was no hand at fishing in the dark. A decent honest man I thought him. He set me on my way at first light—and never so much as asked me to keep quiet about our meeting." The man's voice still reflected the boy's bursting pride in that instinctive trust. "I hope he got safe away, though of course I never dared to enquire."

He fell silent a little while, wondering what had become of the rough-visaged kindly fellow who had heartened and fed a frightened youngster and then had faded into limbo. Instinctively he had known that any attempt to succour the outlaw could only add to his danger. He hoped that the man had made good his escape to the Americas and had there found a new life for himself.

He roused himself to refill the girls' glasses, despite their doubts, assuring them gravely that he had never entertained so sober a pair. Perhaps it was the unaccustomed wine that inspired Deborah to ask her new sister to dance for them. "Just a few steps," she pleaded, "so that Marc may see for himself how beautiful it is—and not in the least improper as I had been led to believe."

It was certainly the champagne, allied to certain other heady delights that had touched her for the first time that night, that prompted Fleur's consent. "But it will have to be something very slow and stately," she stipulated, looking thoughtfully at the voluminous folds of her dress. "A pavane," she decided. "That would be in keeping with the costume. But it will be icy cold in the nursery and I *must* have music."

"No need to disturb yourself, my dear," said Marcus easily. "It shall be here, and I will play for you, once the covers are drawn, if you will excuse me briefly."

While Reeves performed his duties with professional imperturbability, Deborah looked at Fleur owl-eyed. "I do believe he's going to play his fiddle for you," she breathed. "He's not done that for years. I'm beginning to wonder if you're a witch!"

Below stairs, Reeves came in with the air of a man who knows much, and is prepared, if suitably approached, to divulge just a hint of what he knows. The cook was cross. Despite his best endeavours, three healthy young people had eaten shamefully little. Reeves smiled at him kindly and spoke portentous words.

"To them as knows what I does, that's the best noos I've heard this month past. We've all known, thanks to that there Betty," his tone was nicely calculated to depress the pretensions of one so junior and, worse, so undiscriminating as to share her knowledge with the entire domestic staff, "that things weren't just as they should be." The austerity with which he had enunciated the final phrase melted. He beamed. "Well now I'll have *my* say. *Who* doesn't trouble themselves to eat their victuals? Specially such victuals as *you* provides for 'em, Perry," he added generously. "Only them as is sickly—which even Miss Deborah can't be scarcely so described these weeks past but not in the way of eating hearty, and them as is in love—which young master and missus is *now,* even if they wasn't afore, and that I'll swear to."

After which triumphant peroration he subsided slightly and informed the housekeeper in an under-voice that things at Blayden might now be expected to look up, which it was time they did, and no mistake.

It was some little time before Marcus came back to the library, but when he did, he was indeed carrying a violin. His face was rueful. "Sadly neglected," he told them. "I have done my best with it, and it may endure for one pavane. Shall we adventure?"

He raised an enquiring eyebrow at Fleur, who, flown with sartorial success and champagne, smiled, nodded, and moved out on to the clear space of floor. It took him a moment or two to get the slow duple rhythm while she waited quietly, marking the beat with one slender foot. Then he began to play an old country air. She nodded him the tiniest acknowledgement and swept into the stately measure.

Head bent to his instrument, Marcus watched with deep surprise and admiration. He had not expected such artistry. The dance itself was simple enough. A child could have learned it. But the fluid grace with which it was performed, the eloquence of each slight gesture, were a revelation. It seemed to him that the dancer was possessed, to her very fingertips, by her own art. Even, he thought fancifully, to the tiniest tendril of the shining dark hair. Caught up in the rapture of the dance, she had completely forgotten the watchers. It was an exquisite performance——and he was not at all sure that he liked it.

As she sank in the deep final curtsy Deborah broke the spell with a tiny patter of applause. His wife raised her bowed head with a look in her eyes as of a sleeper awakening and smiled up at him, a child again, looking hopefully for a word of approbation.

He gave it generously as he took her hands to lift her to her feet. "My dear, you will take Almack's by storm. Your dancing is quite delightful. I shall certainly have to polish up my own performance if I am not utterly to disgrace my partner. And I had thought myself no mean exponent, either," he added with a rueful twinkle.

Her eyes were like stars, "Almack's!" she breathed. "Will you really take me there?"

"But of course! It is *de rigeur* for a bride making her début. If you cannot obtain vouchers for Almack's you are nobody. Luckily we can rely on my father for that. I believe he calls cousins with Mrs. Burrell, and she will undoubtedly bring the other partonesses round her finger."

"Soon? Shall we go soon?" she begged, lost in roseate dreams.

"I thought perhaps we might set out next week and take the journey easily, since we must rely on hirelings. There is no vast hurry. The season has scarce begun. But you will wish to rig yourself out in town finery before you make any formal appearances. At least you need not trouble your head with domestic responsibilities. We must put up at a hotel, since my lodging in the Albany is too small to house us. Next year we must think about hiring a house for the season, but it is too late for this year."

She sank down on a low stool on the hearth, her eyes wide and eager. This was the first indication he had given that he meant to take her with him when he left Blayden. So that he did *that*, she did not greatly care where they went. He could immure her in the Kentish manor or instal her in shabby-genteel lodgings in the suburbs for all she cared! Almack's? All the pleasures of the season? Why—yes—for just so long as Marcus was there too.

He began to detail some of the treats in store, his rather harsh features considerably softened by kindly amusement. The girls listened, Deborah wistfully, Fleur more interested in the speaker than in his tale. Neither of them heard the distant door bell, though Marcus noted it with mild annoyance. Just the one night when he would prefer *not* to have belated guests. And a queer time of night for anyone to be calling, even if it *was* the full of the moon.

Reeves, entering presently, proffered a visiting card on his calver and announced austerely, "The gentleman sent his apologies for calling upon you at such an unseasonable hour, sir, but he has come post from London. He says that his business is most urgent and will brook no delay."

Marcus picked up the card. Fleur, watching him, saw his face change. All the kindliness, all the animation that had so softened his expression, were wiped away, and there sat the cool, arrogant stranger of their first meeting. She shrank a little, her own warm happiness dimmed, and wondered who was the visitor who had wrought this disastrous change. But it seemed that he was a friend.

"Harry Redfern!" exclaimed Marcus. "I'd best see what brings him in such haste. And Reeves— see what refreshment Mrs. Bresson can arrange for him. If he has come post he can't have dined." And excusing himself to the girls, he went off to greet his guest.

Fleur's pretty lips drooped disconsolately. It had been such a wonderful evening—quite the happiest of her short married life—and now it was all spoiled by this intrusive stranger who would probably stay for hours.

But here she was mistaken. It was not even a quarter of an hour before Marcus was back, bringing with him a pleasant-faced if weary-looking young man whom he introduced as his friend Mr. Redfern. "I brought him to you straight," he explained, in tacit apology for the visitor's travel-stained condition, "that he may make my excuses. The news he brings is of the gravest. Napoleon has escaped from Elba and landed in France, where, if report speaks truth, he is being welcomed right joyfully. Harry reckons he will be in Paris by now. You will forgive me, my dears, but I must set out at once. This means war again, and everyone who can help in any way will be needed." He turned to Fleur. "It grieves me that I must, after all, leave you behind, but I know that you will understand. With good fortune our separation may not be for long. I will send you word as soon as it is possible for you to join me. Meanwhile, if you will see to it that Harry has something to eat, I will go make my own preparations."

In numb misery Fleur watched him go. The cup of happiness had been snatched from her lips before she had done more than taste. All her dreams, all their fine plans, must be cast aside because once more the ogre was loose. But why must Marcus go, she thought resentfully. He was not a soldier. He would probably call himself a farmer, since she had learned in recent weeks that he gave a good deal more of his time and his energy to his acres than was usual with the landed gentry. And how could a farmer help the progress of a war?

It was some small comfort to be called into Marcus's room, where he had hastily flung a few necessities into a valise, and asked to take charge of such gear as he must leave behind. At least it made her feel that she had *some* part in his life, albeit a small one.

His preparations complete, he turned to her at last, where she stood hesitating by the doorway. "We shall be leaving as soon as Harry has eaten," he said gently. "Be a good child while I am gone. Amuse yourself with the new furnishings and look after Deb for me." He set his hands on her shoulders, stooped and kissed her lips. A grave,

gentle kiss, very different from those that he had
bestowed upon her only an hour or two earlier. She
knew herself already half forgotten in the urgency
of his new preoccupation, and struggled valiantly to
hold back the tears that threatened.

He understood in part. "Don't come downstairs
again," he said kindly. "I will make your excuses to
Harry."

She nodded and turned away blindly, fumbling
for a handkerchief. When she looked up again he
was gone. For the second time in her married life,
Mrs. Blayden cried herself to sleep.

Pounding steadily southward, her husband was
aware, despite his deep concern with matters of
national import, of an odd regret, almost an ache,
for the parting with his wife. He had not thought
to miss her so. Sometime during the night watches,
the exhausted Harry heavily asleep in his corner of
the chaise, he found himself recalling an old jingle
with which his nurse had been used to admonish
him when he had scorned or rejected some offered
treat. How did the thing go? Presently it came back
to him.

> *He who will not when he may,*
> *When he will, he shall have nay.*

In the darkness he smiled a little. She was his
wife. When the time came to claim her there could
be no question of 'Nay'.

EIGHT

TEMPESTUOUS spring gave way to sober summer. In the isolation of Blayden it was difficult to keep in touch with what was happening in the wider world, but occasional rumours reached the ears of two anxious girls, even in their quiet backwater. The neighbourhood was in a ferment of activity. Several youngsters who had frequently bemoaned the fate that had caused them to be born just too late to have a crack at Boney hurried off to enlist. The price of horses and fodder began to mount. The more sober citizens busied themselves in seeing that the warning beacons, neglected in recent months, were put in readiness once more.

Finding that only the more alarming rumours survived long enough to reach them, Fleur formed the habit of riding over to High Barrows almost daily. Grandpapa had the *London Gazette* sent to him regularly, so one could be sure of reliable news only four or five days old. He also had unofficial sources of information through the channels of commerce, though these were not entirely to be trusted. Grandpapa, unfortunately, was in his blackest mood. He denounced the incompetence that had permitted Bonaparte to escape with a fury that empurpled his face and knotted its muscles into an awesome mask. The shuffling efforts of the French royalists and the king's final flight to Ghent provoked another outburst. The good humour that had radiated from him on his grand-daughter's wedding day might never have existed. So savage was his temper that his entire household seemed to exist on tiptoe, creeping about with bated breath and giving each other warning of his approach with small significant jerks of the head so that fellow sufferers might take action to avoid the oncoming fury. And even this did not always save them, since he was just as likely to erupt into wrath at finding some hapless wretch absent from his allotted place of duty.

But the worst explosion of all was caused by his granddaughter. He had seemed calmer that morning, so that she was quite unprepared for the scene that followed. Apparently busy with his accounts, he allowed her to read the latest reports without interruption. A cautious comment on the interesting potentialities of Captain Whinyates's rockets as an artillery unit was received with nothing more alarming than a sour grunt. But as she rose to go he swung round on his chair and jerked out sharply, "Married in February, wasn't you? And no expense spared. A pretty penny that cost me, first and last. Well—now it's May. What about it, my girl? Are you in the family way or are you not?" He eyed her slight body with a fulminating glare that clearly indicated his expectation of disappointment, and swept on bitterly, "And if you're not, what does that idle, expensive young whippersnapper mean by jauntering off to London? I've paid down my blunt like an honest man and I'll not have him shabbing off till I see you in a promising way to giving me something for my money."

Perhaps it was the suddenness of the attack; perhaps it was the freedom of speech that she had enjoyed since her marriage. For the first time in her life Fleur was not petrified by one of Grandpapa's rages—and she was quite as angry as he was.

"In that case you should have had your stipulations written into the marriage contract before you signed me away," she flashed back at him. "No. I am not in the family way. Nor like to be, since my husband puts his duty to his country before the breeding of heirs just to satisfy *your* vanity." And then, with a pride that certainly smacked of insolence, "Did you really believe that your gold could

chain him to my side when honour demanded that
he go?"

They were brave words, loyal words, but they
were disastrous. No one had dared to cross his will
for years, and that now it should be the mongrel
French brat that he had taken in, he persuaded himself, out of charity, seemed to him the ultimate in-
sult. It was several minutes before he could master
himself sufficiently to speak, and when he did his
speech was heavy and slow, lacking its old brisk
resonance.

"Fine words, aren't they, missy? 'Duty' and 'honour' and 'love of country'. It hasn't taken the gentry
long to teach you their glib parrot phrases. Sound
better than what it says in the Bible about honour-
ing your parents—*and* your grandparents, that
have taken you in and fed you and clothed you for
nigh on fifteen years. Well—you'll find out soon
enough that fine words butter no parsnips; and fine
lords are just as fond of gold as honest merchants
—only they don't like working for it. Take yourself off. And don't put yourself about to come back
until you've given me the great-grandchild I'm waiting for. From today my doors are closed to you."

Fleur stared at him in mingled shock and penitence. There was a pathetic dignity about him at
that moment that made her deeply ashamed of her
outburst. Had she not been miserable and anxious
herself, she thought, she would never have spoken
so. But *he* had said unforgivable things, too. Besides, she knew from past experience that while

he was in this mood, apology would be useless.

"As you wish, sir," she said formally, curtsied, and left him.

Once or twice before he had uttered preposterous threats during his fits of rage. When the fit had passed—it might be a day or so, or even as long as a week—the threats were forgotten. He never mentioned them again and, of course, he never apologised. But this was the first time that she had been the direct cause of his anger. She thought she had best give him a day or two to cool down and then try to discover how the land lay. But before she could put this plan into action, one of the grooms from High Barrows brought her a letter. It was not, as she had first surmised, from her grandfather, but from Mr. Willets, his man of business. And before she had time to break the seal the bearer gave her a very good notion of its contents by tugging at his forelock and mumbling, "Please, miss—ma'am, I *should* say—will you show me where I'm to put the horses?" and glancing up in bewilderment she saw that a regular cavalcade was coming up the avenue.

Her beloved Chérie had been stabled at Blayden ever since her marriage, but here were all the other horses that she had ever ridden, even the old grey pony, her very first mount, long since outgrown.

"Master said to tell you they wasn't going to be a charge on him no more," muttered the groom shamefacedly, softening the message as much as he dared, for Mr. Pennington had given it in consider-

ably more picturesque detail. "The saddles and such
are all in the wagon with the rest of your things
that he told Maria to pack up. They've fallen a bit
behind."

She showed him where the horses could be
turned loose in the home paddock for the present,
and then dismissed him to the kitchen quarters to
refresh himself, managing to speak quietly and
pleasantly and even to summon a smile as she
thanked him. There was room and to spare in the
Blayden stables, though extra hands would be
needed. That was a business that she would tackle
later. First she must find some private place where
she could read the lawyer's letter undisturbed.

It was, in essence, a legal repetition of her grandfather's final threat. She was forbidden to com-
municate with him, either in person or by letter,
until she had fulfilled the conditions of which, said
Mr. Willets, his client had assured him that she was
fully cognisant.

If it had not been staring at her in black and
white, Fleur would not have believed it. To be sure,
she had spoken hastily—yes, she would admit it—
even rudely, but it had been in defence of her husband. And Grandpapa had never been one to care
overmuch for hard words. Not realising the intensity of his obsession with that unborn great-grandchild, she could not understand why, this time, he
was harbouring so bitter a grievance.

She was not very old. Hard on the heels of shock
and dismay came resentment. She closed her mind

to the knowledge that she was in part to blame for the breach between them, hardened her heart, and determined to show Grandpapa how little she cared for his intransigent attitude.

She found that she *did* care, a good deal more than she had expected. It was not that she was attached to Grandpapa. He had never invited affection or sought to win it. But High Barrows was still home. At Blayden she had no duties, no responsibilities; indeed, with Marcus gone, no place. She had grown fond of Deborah, but the girl's sickly habit had naturally inclined her towards quiet indoor pursuits, whereas Fleur's vigorous health demanded more active occupation. She put in a good deal of time with her horses, grooming, exercising, schooling. She unpacked, arranged and re-arranged all the belongings that Grandpapa had sent over from High Barrows. Some of the items she had almost forgotten—a sampler with sadly crooked stitches that she had made when she was seven; the coral and bells given to her in babyhood by her long-dead Papa. Grandpapa had certainly made a clean sweep, she thought ruefully!

To add to her feeling of rootlessness, she had so far received only two letters from her husband. The first was written soon after his arrival in London, telling her that, for the present, she should write to him at his lodging in the Albany. He went on to describe the queer state of affairs in Town—a few devoted patriots wholly engaged in preparations for war, but most of society enjoying the

pleasures of the season as though they had not a
care in the world. He signed himself her affectionate
husband, but there was no other suggestion of personal feeling in the letter. She told herself that he
was very busy with more urgent matters; that gentlemen did not care for writing letters and were not
good at expressing their softer emotions. She read
and re-read the precious missive until she had its
few brief sentences by heart. Finally, with much
pen nibbling and a sadly wasteful rejection of half-
written pages, she wrote her reply. Because she
had her pride, she would not write to him of her
loneliness. The letters were simple factual accounts
of the small happenings of her daily life, such
letters as she might well have written to her mother.
But writing seemed to bring him closer, so as soon
as one letter was safely dispatched she would begin
upon the next, and as the days went by with no
answer to her regular screeds, she blamed her disappointment on bad roads or dishonest mail
carriers.

The second letter arrived at the end of May. It
was longer than the first and opened very pleasantly.
He had been out of Town for a while, delayed
longer than he had expected, and had found several
letters from his wife awaiting his return. He thanked
her for them and said how comfortable it was to
have the news of home. He was thankful that she
and Deborah were safe in peaceful Blayden. Here,
in Town tension was rising. For his part he was
perfectly confident of the final outcome of the con-

flict, but there was a good deal of doubt and anxiety, even in well-informed circles, because of the inexperience of many of the allied troops. She would understand that everyone must give what help they could, and it had been suggested to him that his fluent French, together with a smattering of Flemish and German, would be useful to those who were trying to pull a very polyglot army into some kind of shape. There was no cause for alarm. He was *not* enlisting and would take good care to keep clear of the fighting when it began, but he was leaving for Brusssels almost at once. He would do his best to write to her, but since the mail services were in chaos because of the demands of military traffic she was not to fret if the letters did not get through. He sent an affectionate message to Deborah and trusted that the two of them were keeping out of mischief during his absence.

He had, of course, protested his safety and his excessive caution too much. It was entirely out of character with all that she knew of him. Not the most indifferent of wives could keep from worrying under these circumstances, and Fleur was miserably uneasy. Since communications with High Barrows had ceased she had spent three intolerable days without news and had then arranged with Reeves to have a newspaper brought up to the house each day. But there was little information to be gained from its columns, which seemed to be largely devoted to social gossip. So far as she could see, Brussels had become the new centre of society.

London must be deserted, for everyone was going
to Belgium to see the sights and to indulge in re-
views and riding parties, cricket matches and balls,
and, no doubt, delightful flirtations. The one letter
that she received from her husband during this
period certainly supported this view. He mentioned
several of these festive occasions, presumably with
the idea of setting her mind at rest as to his personal
safety. But he also said that she had been much in
his mind of late since he had been staying in the
neighbourhood of Fleurus. Not that the place lived
up to its charming name, its dominant feature being
a brickworks, but nevertheless the name had set him
to recalling their first meeting and how he had
called her a 'flower of France'.

Not a very loverlike epistle, one would say. But it
was the best she had had of him and she savoured
it to the full, extracting every scrap of comfort from
the meagre phrases. She was a little puzzled as to
what he could be doing in Fleurus. It was not the
first time that she had heard of the place. Maman,
who had grown up in the border country, had also
told her about the town that had a name so like
hers. She had even mentioned the brickworks,
which had a tower, remembered Fleur, that could
be seen from miles around. But she had thought
Fleurus was in France. Certainly it was a long way
from Brussels. She went down to the library and
spent an hour seeking for any book or map that
might mention it, but there was nothing. Not that
it was important, of course, but knowing just were

it was would make her feel closer to Marcus.

Before she had time to wear this third missive to shreds or to find out any more details about the town of Fleurus, every thought of it was quite driven from her head by the receipt of shocking news from High Barrows. It was Mr. Pennington's habit to deal with his correspondence and read his newspapers in the library before partaking of his dinner, which he still took, following the custom of his youth, at three o'clock in the afternoon. Since he was a hearty trencherman, his household was a little surprised when he did not emerge from his seclusion in good time for this repast, but such had been his temper of late that no one dared to disturb him to draw his attention to the time.

Consequently it was close upon six before a trembling footman, the lowest in the domestic hierarchy who could not delegate the perilous task to anyone else, was sent to attend to the library fire and to discover the body of his master slumped over the writing table. A physician, summoned in frantic haste, pronounced upon examination that his patient had suffered a severe apoplectic seizure. He would let him some blood and apply a blister to his head to draw out the poisons from the brain, but, he shook his head gravely, the prognosis was not hopeful. It was a pity that he had not been summoned sooner. He proceeded to instruct the frightened servants as to his needs and wishes.

Robert Pennington died that night—spared the tortures of the prescribed treatment, which was

more mercy than had been granted to his miserable
monarch. The news of his death was brought to
his grand-daughter next morning, together with an
urgent request from Mr. Willets that she should
return immediately to High Barrows.

NINE

"FIFTEEN pounds a year?" Fleur looked dazed, pinched and plain in her mourning.

Mr. Willets gave the deferential little bob of his head that would have been a bow had he been standing. "That is the figure, ma'am. I was to inform you that this was the amount, together with board and lodging, that he paid his housekeeper, and that your husband could supply the board and lodging. Also that, if you wished to better your position, you knew how to set about it." He sighed his relief for the ending of his unpleasant duty and became again a human being, kindly and concerned for the girl he had known from childhood. "Believe

me, Miss Fleur, I did my utmost to persuade him.
I told him that it was unjust. How could you—how
could *any* woman—be certain that she would be
blessed with children?"

Even in her stunned disbelief, Fleur found that
mildly funny. Mrs. Willets, at least, was numbered
among the elect. At the last count the Willets pro-
geny had numbered eight, and another 'blessing'
was imminent.

"He would not listen to reason," sighed the unhappy little man. "You know what he was like,
Miss Fleur, when he took a notion."

Fleur did. It was hard to believe that all that
fierce determination had been stilled, laid to rest
in quiet earth only yesterday.

"If he had lived I am convinced that he would
have revoked this iniquitous disposition," continued
Mr. Willets earnestly. "I had already persuaded him
to agree that the capital should devolve upon you
on your thirty-fifth birthday, if at that date you
were without issue."

"Thirty-five," said Fleur thoughtfully. She was
seventeen and a half. A whole lifetime away. Had
he arrived at that figure by simple multiplication?
Or had he reckoned that by then she would be past
child bearing? In any case, it was of academic
interest only. Save for bequests to servants and the
fifteen pounds a year to his grand-daughter, the
bulk of his fortune was left in trust for his first-
born great-grandson, provided that the names
Robert Pennington were bestowed upon the infant

at his baptism. There was provision for the upkeep of High Barrows and for the retention of the services of Mr. Willets. All other income from the trust was at the free use and discretion of the parents of the said infant until he attained his twenty-fifth birthday, when it would pass into his own control. Robert Pennington had certainly had the last word!

Poor Mr. Willets! She spared a thought from her own problems for the poor little man's obvious misery. He was still fidgeting with his papers, his burden not yet fully discharged. What more could there be?

"There is just one other matter, ma'am," he said, suddenly remembering her changed status. "These letters." He brought out a bundle of letters, many of them of some age, though one or two looked fresh and clean. And now he was looking anywhere but straight at her. "In the course of my duties I went through the contents of Mr. Pennington's safe cabinet. I found these. Upon glancing through them—as I was obliged to do," he explained in deep embarrassment, "I found that they had been written by Mrs. Alexander Pennington—your mother. I felt it only right that you should be informed of their existence and their contents. If, when you have read them, you would care to consult me as to your possible actions, I shall be very happy to advise to the best of my ability."

Fleur did her best to say all that was polite and appreciative, but her eyes were all for the letters,

her heart hungry for news, at last, of Maman. News
which, by the appearance of the bundle, had been
accumulating for some years.

She carried them up to her own room and chose
one at random. It had been written three years ago
and it was a touching appeal for news of her beloved daughter. Enclosed within it and unopened
was a note addressed to herself.

By the time that she had read it, tears were
rolling down Fleur's cheeks, though whether they
were for sorrow or for happiness she could scarcely
have said. Perhaps they were just the melting of
the icy barrier of distrust that had grown up when
she felt herself deserted. For the note breathed
affection and tender concern in every syllable. Hastily she searched through the other letters. In all
but two there was a similar unopened note. She
read them all, slowly, thoughtfully, rejoicing for
herself yet grieving for poor darling Maman, who,
happy as she was in her second marriage, still
yearned for news of the little daughter whom she
loved so dearly.

At last she put the notes aside and briefly
scanned the letters that had been addressed to
Grandpapa. They all followed much the same pattern save for the two most recent, and it seemed
unlikely that they had received any reply. But one
letter, some six months old, was an appeal for
financial help. The ache of tears in the girl's throat
became almost unbearable as she read the pathetic
attempt at dignity that scarcely veiled a desperate

need. Her husband, said Maman, had broken his wrist and had been unable to work for several weeks. Care was still needed if he was to regain the full use of the injured member so essential to a musician. Would Mr. Pennington consider making them a small temporary loan against the security of the house in Hans Town?

As Fleur unfolded the last letter of the bundle a fifty-pound bill dropped out and fluttered almost unheeded to the floor. The letter was brief. Maman was returning the money he had sent. Under no circumstances would she agree to his suggestion that she should resign her rights as her daughter's natural guardian. Despite their long separation, which she had accepted solely for Fleur's benefit, the child was most dear to her. Indeed, as soon as circumstances permitted, she proposed to journey north to see for herself that all was well with the girl.

Fleur had a tremulous little smile for that brave bit of gasconade. Darling Maman! Who was undoubtedly shabby and probably hungry, and who certainly had no money for coach fares!

But it was no smiling matter. The letter was dated for the twenty-fourth of January and there had been nothing since. A hasty count suggested that the letters had been coming roughly every three months, so the silence was a long one, and, in the circumstances, worrying. She must write at once and tell Maman what had happened to the letters and assure her of her love. And also to tell her of

Grandpapa's death. Maman did not read English very easily and might well miss the announcement in the papers.

Once started, it was difficult to stop. She had covered several pages when she suddenly realised that she had not yet told Maman that she was married. It would really be very much easier to go and see her and explain everything in person. The idea was an attractive one, but the thought of fifteen pounds a year put it out of court. Perhaps Marcus would take her to visit Maman when she joined him in London. With a sharp little sigh she wondered how much longer she would have to wait before he sent for her.

There had been no time, since Grandpapa's sudden death, for following the war news in the papers. Vaguely she had heard that fighting had begun and that the allied armies had met with a sharp reverse at a place called Ligny. Mr. Willets had told her that there had been some very gloomy faces over *that* among the gentlemen who had attended Grandpapa's funeral. Perhaps it would all be over soon and Marcus could come home.

She put her letter aside for a while and went to sit with Deborah, stooping as she left the room to pick up the forgotten fifty-pound bill and tuck it back into the envelope from which it had fallen and thinking as she did so that it was very unlike Grandpapa to have overlooked it.

She found Deborah poring over the paper, her face flushed and excited. As Fleur came in she cried out eagerly. "My love, I was just about to send Betty to find you. There has been a great battle. Napoleon has been beaten and the French armies are in retreat. I don't understand it very well, but the paper says it is a great victory for the Duke of Wellington." She smiled up at Fleur happily. "Now Marcus can come home and we may all be happy and comfortable once more."

In their delight and relief at the splendid news, neither girl gave a thought to the tragic cost of that victory, but it was different when day by day the newspapers printed their stories of heroism and tragedy. The Duke's own despatch, speaking of the army's immense losses, abated their first joy. Foolishly they had imagined that, in a battle, the losses of the winning side would be comparatively few. The casualty lists horrified them, even in their ignorance of the awful sufferings of the wounded and the appallingly high death rate in the hastily improvised hospitals.

And still there was no word from Marcus. Fleur was restless and uneasy, but not yet deeply anxious. Common sense told her that he could not immediately desert his post, whatever it was, just because the battle was won. There must be, in homely domestic terms, a great deal of tidying up to be done. As for delays in the arrival of letters, that, too, was only to be expected. So she endured with reasonable fortitude, bewailing the interminable waiting no more than three or four times a day to Deborah, who, in any case, was of like mind.

Until the day when, in one of the accounts of battle, her eye caught the familiar name Fleurus. Startled, she read on, and learned for the first time that the place had been in the very thick of the fighting. Why, Napoleon himself had used the tower of the brickfield as an observation post during the battle of Ligny and had passed the following night in the town! All this she read with whitening cheeks, only half comprehending because somewhere inside her a voice was saying, "But Marcus was there—in Fleurus. And it's not only soldiers who get hurt or killed when there's fighting. Other people can get wounded too. Marcus! No. Please, God, no! Not Marcus!"

But while a frantic child stammered her incoherent prayer for her husband's safety, the decisiveness and organising ability inherent in Robert Pennington's grandchild, nourished by close association with him, sprang to action. She rang for Betty, and by the time that the girl came in was ready with a string of calm orders that seemed to form themselves in her mind without her own volition.

"Have Tompson saddle up Brutus and ride over to High Barrows. He is to ask Mr. Willets to wait upon me here this afternoon on a matter of grave urgency. Then he is to go on to Penrith and book two seats on the London Mail. Tomorrow's, if they have vacancies. Do you wish to go with me to London, Betty? If you do not, I will take Emily. It will not be a very comfortable journey since we are not travelling post."

Betty, eagerly protesting her entire indifference to such minor matters as personal comfort, was silenced, not unkindly. "Very well, then. Pack what we shall need for a stay of several weeks. My plainest gowns. I am going to visit my mama, who lives very quietly. Now I must go up to Miss Deborah. No. Wait. Tompson will need money for the tickets."

From the locked drawer of her bureau she took the bundle of letters. Though she had had little cause for spending since she came to Blayden, there were not many coins left in her purse. Swiftly she extracted the fifty-pound bill and handed it to Betty. At that moment she would have turned highwayman without hesitation if by so doing she could put herself in the way of getting news of Marcus.

Now for the more difficult task of explaining the situation to Deborah without alarming her too much about her brother's safety.

Deborah protested and pleaded and even wept a little, but was firmly if gently overborne by this newly determined Fleur. Mr. Willets was gravely concerned. So young a child to embark on so long a journey with no better protection than the country-bred Betty. Yet he admitted that she had real cause for anxiety and sympathised with her desire for action. He would have offered his own escort save that Mrs. Willets's delicate situation made it impossible for him to leave her at this present. What troubled him most was that Fleur had received no reply to the letter that he knew she had sent to her mother. If he could have been assured that she would receive welcome and shelter from Madame de Trèvy—this was Maman's new name—he could have let her go with an easier mind. As matters stood, he felt there was no telling what might have become of that lady. The family might have removed to humbler lodgings—might even have returned to France. There were also grimmer possibilities. He did not mention these to a girl who already had a sufficient burden of anxiety, but contented himself with furnishing her with the direction of a respectable hotel where she could be perfectly comfortable and asking if she had ample funds to cover the expenses of the journey.

Fleur told him about the fifty-pound bill. He agreed without a blink that she might quite properly take this money for her own use. But when she explained that, upon reaching London, she intended to sell her pearls in order to replace it, he was quite horrified.

"Indeed, Miss Fleur, you must do no such thing," he insisted. "You would be bound to be cheated. Even a reputable jeweller would offer you less than half their value. He would tell you that pearls were no longer fashionable or some such thing and reckon it no more than fair business dealing. No, no. The sensible thing to do is to deposit the pearls with me. I will advance you the sum that Mr. Pennington paid for them, which I can easily discover from his papers. And when this awkward business is happily cleared up, as I am sure I hope it soon may be, your husband may buy them back for you."

He beamed at her, delighted to have found a way out of the difficulty, and Fleur thanked him gratefully. He then added that, as it would be scarcely prudent for her to carry so large a sum of money on her person while she was exposed to all the mischances of travel, he would give her a letter of credit entitling her to draw upon his partner, Mr. Sickling of Leadenhall Street, for such sums as she required. She thanked him once more for his kindness, begged him to carry her affectionate good wishes to Mrs. Willets, and bade him farewell, saying that she had a great deal to do before tomorrow's early start.

Sipping Lord Blayden's malaga appreciatively, Mr. Willets presently permitted his mouth to relax into a prim little smile of satisfaction at his own simple cunning. Bless the child! She had never even suspected that the fifty-pound bill had been of his providing. Since her grandfather had remembered *him* with surprising generosity, he could well afford it. He had even toyed with the idea of making it a hundred, but had come to the regretful conclusion that no one who had known the late Mr. Pennington would believe that he had casually overlooked a sum of *that* magnitude! He felt that he was now in the happy position of being able to ensure that the provisions of her grandfather's will did not bear too harshly on his young client.

His smile faded. There could be no denying that, as an executor, he had failed in his duty of carrying out the testator's intentions. Nor could he comfort himself with a pious hope that, wherever he was, the testator might by now have changed his mind. That seemed to him highly unlikely. But the estate was not a penny the worse for his dealings, and as for the rest——! He drained his glass, jammed his hat on his head at a positively pugnacious angle, and marched out to his waiting carriage—despite thinning hair and rotund habit, a very perfect gentle knight.

TEN

UNDER other circumstances Fleur would have enjoyed her unexpected journey to London, being young enough to discount cramped and stuffy quarters, hurriedly snatched meals and lack of sleep in return for all the incidental excitements of travel. As it was she paid little heed to the passing scene. The guard, who had accepted the two passengers into his care with genial interest, was sadly disappointed. To be sure, the young lady looked good for a handsome tip and the abigail was just the sort of comely wench that he enjoyed passing the time of day with, but his professional pride was mortified by repeated enquiries as to the day's mileage

and the disappointed air with which his replies were
received. He told the young lady rather huffily that
eight miles an hour was a very good speed on these
roads. And hadn't he his time bill to keep and no
use at all in running ahead of it? Did she want them
all overturned in the ditch? In winter, now she
might have had cause for complaint, what with
mud and icy roads. He would have talked himself
back into good humour, recounting some of the
awful experiences that she would scarcely believe,
but she had already turned away, her shoulders
drooping disconsolately.

Fortunately, a few friendly words with Mistress
Betty the next time that they stopped for a change
of horses restored the situation. The news that her
mistress was hastening to London to seek word of
a husband missing since the great battle immediately
enlisted the guard's sympathies, especially when the
girl confided that the pair had been married but a
few months. After that he quite surpassed himself
in his efforts to secure their comfort, and when at
last they reached Town he did not let them out of
his sight until he had seen them safely into a hackney carriage driven by a respectable cove that he
could vouch for. The tip was all that he had hoped
—Fleur had not yet grown accustomed to her new
poverty—but the gratitude on the two faces meant
more. He cleared his throat, which felt unaccount-
able dry, and stepped into the inn to drain a pint
of porter to the young lady's happy reunion with
her husband.

Fleur's courage failed her a little when they reached Town. She had meant to go straight to Hans Town. But it was late and the streets were so crowded and noisy and even *her* vitality was exhausted by the rigours of travel. She was thankful enough to go to the hotel of Mr. Willets's choosing and have Betty tuck her up in a comfortable bed once more. But a good night's sleep did much to restore her and she was up betimes next day.

With the whole day before her, she decided to call first at her husband's lodging in the Albany. She was a little doubtful of the propriety of this course, but surely a wife might call at her husband's apartments, especially if she was attended by her maid. But the call brought only disappointment. On learning the identity of this very early visitor, Dearden, Mr. Blayden's man, promptly put all the resources of the establishment at her disposal, but he could add nothing to her knowledge of his master's movements. So far as he knew, Mr. Blayden was not yet returned from Belgium. "Though it may be as he's stopped off at Dakers, ma'am," he added, in a kindly attempt at comfort. "He spends a deal of his time there and comes and goes pretty freely between the two."

Fleur sensed that the man himself was a little anxious over the absence of news and liked him the better for it, even though it did nothing to relieve her own fears. She arranged to call again next day and promised to furnish Dearden with her direction as soon as she was fixed in Town, declined an offer of refreshment, glanced about her curiously at this shabbily comfortable masculine stronghold, and returned to the waiting hackney.

Driving back to the hotel she planned her next move. She decided against taking Betty with her on her visit to Hans Town. There could be no reason why a young married lady should not go alone to visit her mother. And if, as seemed probable, Maman was living in humble circumstances, she might not wish to have her poverty exposed to the inquisitive eyes of a stranger. So Betty was left to finish the unpacking and to press the creases from dresses rumpled by travel, with a promise that she should go out to see the sights later.

Anxiety for Marcus was temporarily forgotten as Fleur set out for Hans Town. For the moment she was wholly absorbed in the prospect of seeing Maman again. Her patient Jehu had nodded comprehendingly when she gave him the address. "I knows it right enough, Mum," he said comfortably. "It's Chelsea way. Runs off Sloane Street, up by Hans Place."

The names meant nothing to Fleur save that she gathered from the man's manner that the district was perfectly respectable. She looked about her with interest and thought how strange it would be if she should chance to see Maman strolling along the flag walk. But there were few pedestrians about. Fleur, who was already finding London's July heat quite excessive, decided that they must all be enjoying the cool freshness of the neat little gardens that looked so gay and so well tended.

Insensibly her spirits began to rise. At times she had pictured Maman as living in the direst poverty in some dreadful back slum. But this was a charming place. When at last the carriage stopped she jumped out eagerly, desiring her driver to wait for a few minutes until she had ascertained that Madame de Trèvy still lived here. Breathless with excitement, she pulled the bell. She could hear its hollow jangling away at the back of the house, but there was no response to its summons. She rang again, and stepped back a pace, studying the general appearance of the little house. At close quarters it was definitely shabby, clean and neat but sadly in need of a coat of paint, while the curtains, close drawn against the sunlight, were well darned and very faded. Somewhere in the house a baby cried. She raised her hand to try the bell just once more, and as she did so heard halting footsteps within the house. Then the door was flung open and an indignant voice said, "Can you not wait a little moment? I tell you I cannot—"

The voice stopped on an indrawn breath. Fleur, completely taken aback, stared blankly at a slenderly-built middle-aged gentleman who was clutching a baby rather awkwardly in one arm while he held the door open with his other hand, and who looked just as surprised at seeing Fleur as she was at seeing him. Rather absurdly, she had never pictured anyone other than Maman answering her

ring, while the gentleman had obviously been expecting a different caller.

He was the first to recover. "A thousand pardons,
mademoiselle," he said contritely, sketching a comical little bow over the top of the baby's head. "I
was expecting the nurse. You wish to see Madame
de Trèvy, is it not?"

As thankfulness at his words brought a smile to
the anxious young face, his glance sharpened. He
clapped a hand to his head, much to the discom-
posure of the infant, exclaiming, "Crétin! Imbécile!
Mai c'est la petite Fleur, n'est ce pas?" And then,
recollecting himself, "You are my stepdaughter,
Fleur Pennington, are you not? No other could so
resemble my Martine! You say in your letter that
you will visit us soon. And there is not even the
time to answer it, with Martine brought to bed so
suddenly. And this—" proudly he held out the
infant—"is your new little brother. Monsieur Raoul
Henri de Trèvy, entirely at your service."

Between the surprise at his news and the rapidity
with which he was pouring it out, Fleur was beginning to feel quite dazed. Before she could speak
he was off again, miscalling himself for keeping her
standing on the doorstep when she must be longing
to see her Maman, and begging her to enter with an
empressement that would have beseemed an emperor in the forecourt of his palace. She managed
to break in upon this hospitable flow for long
enough to request him to dismiss the waiting carriage, whereupon he thrust the baby into her arms

and went off to bestow a quite unnecessary douceur upon the driver who had already been well paid. Little wonder that the family was in financial straits if her step-papa was always so open-handed. She snuggled the baby's downy head under her chin, a warm amused affection for its father already springing to life within her.

The next hour was one of those halcyon periods than come so rarely once childhood is left behind. In the happiness of Maman's rapturous welcome the other anxieties that pressed upon her daughter receded still further into the background. It was only after an hour spent in a breathless and impassioned exchange of news, in which no one item was completely detailed before the next had thrust it aside, that Fleur, suddenly aware of Maman's pallor and exhaustion, called a halt.

It had already emerged that Maman had been very ill after the birth of the baby a month ago, an illness which she shrugged off laughingly as the penalty of advancing years. She looked very frail now that the flush of excitement had faded, and the reason, thought Fleur shrewdly, was more likely lack of proper nourishment. Yet she was obviously blissfully happy. Her husband openly adored her, and the arrival of the little son, so unexpected after seven years of marriage, had set the crown on their happiness. Nothing, now, would do for them but that Fleur should remove from her hotel and come to them at once. It was a pity that there was no room for the maid, but there were only the two spare bedchambers and Grandpère had one of them. If Fleur really could not dispense with the girl's services then perhaps one of the neighbours might be persuaded to accommodate her, but otherwise she should be sent back to High Barrows.

"Blayden," corrected Fleur unthinkingly. Maman looked surprised, M. de Trèvy amused and interested.

"What are you doing with one of the maids from Blayden?" asked Maman curiously. "Never tell me that starched up icicle lent you one to play duenna out of sheer neighbourliness!" Maman's metaphors, if sadly mixed, were undoubtedly descriptive.

Why had she ever imagined that it would be easier to tell Maman about her marriage when they met, rather than to write about it? It was by far more difficult. They were both looking at her, surprise and curiosity writ plain on their faces.

"Because Blayden is my home," she said baldly, and stretched out her left hand, peeling off her glove for their inspection of her wedding ring. "I was married to Marcus Blayden in February."

To say that this blunt announcement produced dismay and confusion is an understatement. Maman went, if possible, paler than ever. "Married? To a Blayden?" she whispered in shocked tones. "No! And no and no. Sold, we shall say. And if you are married, where then is your husband?"

M. de Trèvy, less emotional but more damning, exclaimed, "Married to *that* one! That man-of-the-town! That acknowledged rake!"

It was Maman's question that Fleur, bewildered and distressed by this hostile reception of her news, answered. "I do not know *where* he is. He went to Belgium. He was in Fleurus. Perhaps he is wounded —killed." Her voice broke on a choked sob.

"Or perhaps he is enjoying the embraces of the ravishing mistress that he keeps so secretly hidden away in his Kentish manor," muttered M. de Trèvy in a savage undervoice, forgetting, in the stress of the moment, that his newly acquired daughter was perfectly familiar with the tongue which he had come to regard as a private language between his wife and himself. The pitiful pain in the great grey eyes was his punishment. The girl looked stricken.

"No!" she whispered.

He tried to make amends. "I should not have said it, child. A rumour, no more. I was wrong to repeat it, Foolish, too. For I dare swear that the gentleman who has won the privilege of taking *you* to wife has long forgotten any clandestine attachments that he might have formed in less happy days."

But he had *not* taken her to wife. And that was one secret that she would not tell them. Not even Maman. She said with dignity, "My husband was very kind to me. Naturally, I am concerned about his well-being."

Husband and wife exchanged glances. So she did not love the man to whom she had been given in marriage, kind or not. This was mere loyalty. M. de Trèvy said that no doubt she would soon hear comfortable news of her husband. Meanwhile where else should she stay but with her own family—a family now so complete—parents, son and daughter. And since, at this juncture, the son of the family demanded attention in no uncertain voice, the matter was considered settled.

ELEVEN

Living with Maman, a Maman who grew a little stronger day by day, was just as delightful as Fleur had imagined it. The little house was full of happiness and laughter. Now that his daughter, as he insisted upon calling her, was able to take charge of the household, M. de Trèvy resumed his professional duties. Fleur discovered that he was employed as visiting master of music and Italian at a school for young ladies in Hans Place, though he also had a number of private pupils. Since it was now holiday time, only one or two parlour boarders whose parents resided abroad made any claim on his services as an instructor, but he also gave a good deal of help with accounts and other matters connected with organisation.

"I work there for some time when first I come to England," he explained to Fleur. The proprietor of the establishment, a M. de St. Quentin, himself a refugee from the revolution, had never failed to welcome fellow exiles to his table. Paul de Trèvy had been introduced by friends. An amicable relationship had grown up between the two men, and M. de St. Quentin, finding that de Trèvy was reliable and well accustomed to work, had eventually offered him employment. "I was thankful enough to take anything," he said reminiscently, and fell silent a while.

"How did you escape from France?" asked Fleur, with all the eagerness of a child demanding a story.

He smiled at her affectionately. Bitterness had left him now, cleansed away by the healing power of Martine's love. "I escape because I am too slow to run away," he said. And, at her puzzled face, went on, "We have warning that the mob will come—to kill, to loot, to burn. Not our own people, you understand, but the scum of the cities for the most part, with one or two stupid hot-heads drunk with words. It is a commonplace, so we are prepare. But then it is discover that the horses are all gone. They mean to make sure of us, see you. That is when all the others run away. Me, I am too lame to run. So I hide in the woods. Then I find many people—humble country people, who risk their lives to help me. So, after many months, I come at last to England—and to Chelsea!"

He did not tell her of the appalling fate that had overtaken the runaways, and blessedly, she did not ask. Her thoughts had gone back to the library at Blayden. She was remembering Marcus's tale of the outlawed peasant who had fed and comforted *him*.

Presently she said, "And how did you discover Maman?"

He laughed. "You expect the grand romantic love story, is it not? Alas! It is your grandpère that I discover, at a concert at Ranelagh. In the old days we go on well together. He is lonely. I give up my lodging and go to live with him in Hans Town. It is convenient for my work, it is économique for both of us. So, when the little Fleur is sent to school and my Martine comes home, me voilà!"

To be sure, told so prosaically, it did not sound very romantic. But Fleur already knew her mother's side of the story, and how, at that unexpected meeting, the old childish adoration had sprung to life again, enriched now by suffering, loneliness and loss; even, ironically, by shared poverty. Moreover, she had seen the pair in their daily life. Not an easy one. There had been many set-backs. M. de Trèvy had begun to establish a reputation for himself, in a modest way, as a violinist. The demand for his services at concerts and soirées had been steadily increasing. The accident to his wrist had put a stop to all that and he had been thankful enough to return to teaching at the St. Quentin school. Their

meagre savings were gone and now that there was a
baby to provide for, there could be no denying that
it was make and scrape with them. Yet they were
happy, having each other, meeting each crisis as it
arose in earnest consultation, working together in
unthinking harmony. And Fleur, who had never
lived in a truly happy home before, sunned herself
in the warmth of this one and never missed the
luxuries of High Barrows and Blayden.

She had insisted on paying her share of the household expenses, and, under Maman's tuition, she was
learning to cook and to clean. Had it not been for
the continuing anxiety about her husband and the
grief of being unable to speak of him freely in a
household that wholeheartedly disapproved of her
marriage, her husband and his family, she would
have been as happy as a child playing at house.

During these early days she did not see much
of Grandpère. Grandpère was engaged in the com-
position of a new ballet. Though, as he was the first
to admit, ballet was by far too grand a term for so
simple an affair. Nevertheless, one was still an
artiste. However brief, however simple, it must still
be perfect of its kind.

It was designed to be an added attraction at a
gaming club much patronised by the 'ton'. A most
respectable establishment, run on the lines of a
private house with everything about it of the most
genteel. The owner had hit upon the notion that a
short ballet, performed during the serving of suppers, would be quite a different touch from the

musical entertainment usually offered by rival estab-
lishments, the more so because ballet was becoming
increasingly popular. Martine and Paul were doubtful. Hardened gamsters, they declared, would not
welcome such distraction. M. Lavelle agreed to this,
but pointed out that the hardened gamesters would
come in any case. The idea was to attract the
younger men.

A heated argument then developed to which
Fleur listened with appreciation. Arguments were
frequent in this voluble household. But having been
conducted with passionate intensity, they were then
abandoned and promptly forgotten, so Fleur derived
considerable enjoyment from them. This one was
a three-cornered contest. Martine said indignantly
that it was prostitution of a pure art to produce a
ballet in such a setting, and that, furthermore, she
did not approve of enticing young men into clubs
where they would game away their money. Paul had
no strong feelings on these moral issues, but
doubted the success of such a startling innovation.

M. Lavelle said that no ballet of his production
could do other than add lustre to the reputation of
the art, even if he chose to present it in a debtors'
prison; that young gentlemen who wished to stake
their blunt would undoubtedly do so, and possibly
in some far less reputable club than Mr. Rockstone's; that no one could possibly prophesy what
would or would not take with the fashionables—
witness the fantastic success of Dr. Graham's Temple of Health in its early days; and finally, that since

there was now another and shockingly clamorous mouth to be filled—here he gazed dotingly upon the grandson of whom he was inordinately proud—they needed the money which he was being paid for his services.

This seemed to settle the argument. In complete good humour, Grandpère stumped off to resume his labours.

During her first week in Hans Town, Fleur called each day at the Albany. There was no news. And Dearden was beginning to greet her with an obvious pity that stung her feminine pride. She felt that she presented a humiliating picture of an unwanted wife hanging around her husband's abode in hopes of a kindly word. Moreover, the daily pilgrimage was a costly business since it meant hiring a carriage each time. Her money was melting away with disconcerting speed. Though they lived frugally enough, she found the shops difficult to resist. There were so many trifles, quite inexpensive, that one wanted to buy for a newly acquired family. She had told Maman about Grandpapa's will, though she had not disclosed the exact provisions, saying only that the capital was tied up in trust for her children and that until she was older she had only fifteen pounds a year.

Maman had exclaimed that it was just the kind of Turkish treatment one might have expected from such an old skinflint, but no use to worry one's head about what could not be mended. Grandpère, more worldly wise, grunted, "Meant to make you wholly dependent on your husband, did he? I daresay he made a handsome settlement. Well—he must have done. Stands to reason. The Blaydens wouldn't have condescended to the bourgeoisie without." He pondered this distasteful thought for a moment under frowning brows, then said abruptly. "It's a bad family you're married into, my girl. I don't know the young one, though it's little good I've heard of him, but I've seen enough and to spare of his lordship. He's one that would sell his own daughter for the money to put on a horse." Presently he added heavily, "Seems to me if that husband of yours never *did* come back from Belgium you'd be well clear of an unfortunate coil that never should have been if your Grandfather Pennington had consulted your mother, as was only right."

Fleur's lips drooped. It made her very unhappy when, as so often happened, her family commented unfavourably on her husband. And try as she would, she could not help wondering if there was some foundation for their disapproval, the more so because they were usually fair-minded and tolerant. Grandpère saw the woebegone face and said more cheerfully, "But that's enough about the Blaydens. I've been thinking, my dear, it's time you saw some of the sights of the Town. If tomorrow proves fine, how would it be if you and I went to see those lawyers of yours? We could go by boat, if you'd care for it, and come back by road. That way you'd see everything without getting too tired. And another thing. Why don't you set this Mr. Sickling to making some enquiries about your husband? Or at least arrange for him to take letters and messages for you so that you need not traipse to the Albany every day."

Martine clapped her hands. "An excellent notion, Papa," she approved. "We will make it a feast day, and I shall prepare a special dinner against your return."

So it was settled, and the two intrepid voyagers rose very early next day to be sure of catching the first boat.

Grandpère's knowledge of the passing scene proved, alas, inadequate to his grand-daughter's eager questioning, but fortunately it was amply supplemented by a bevy of helpful passengers. So kind they were to a country ignoramus that Fleur was quite sorry to bid them farewell when she and Grandpère disembarked at London Bridge. Their welcome at the offices of Sickling and Willets was impressive. Whatever her present penury, young Mrs. Blayden was a valuable client. Mr. Sickling was delighted to render every service within his power. But certainly he would accept messages and letters and forward them to Hans Town. And naturally—with a reproachful glance at M. Lavelle, whose suggestion it was—he would not divulge his client's whereabouts to anyone save her husband without her express permission.

Emerging from these solemn precincts, Fleur's purse comfortably plump once more and M. Lavelle delivered from a nightmare vision of an irate Lord

Blayden arriving on his doorstep to demand his errant daughter-in-law, their holiday mood revived. If she would not object to the dust, suggested Grandpère, they might hire an open carriage for their return journey so that she would be able to see everything. Fleur thought this a capital scheme, so after a brief visit to St. Paul's Cathedral, which the girl declared she simply must see since she had heard so much about it, the two adventurers drove gaily off along the Strand in a very shabby landau with the top folded back.

A call at the Albany having produced the usual negative result, Dearden was instructed to send word to Messrs. Sickling and Willets if Mr. Blayden returned. The landau then drove off, leaving the servant to stare after it rather grimly. He couldn't blame her, *that* he couldn't. It didn't seem right to leave the poor young thing in such suspense. No wonder she was getting huffish. Dearden himself, knowing what he knew, was desperately concerned for his master's safety. It was long past time that they should have heard from him. But the orders were that never, whatever the apparent necessity, were enquiries to be made, and he dared not disobey.

It was growing quite late when the aged landau eventually deposited the two travellers at their gate, very well pleased with their adventures and each other, and Fleur bubbling over with eagerness to tell of all that she had seen. It was fortunate, said Maman with pretended severity, that she had decided to make a cassoulet for dinner, since that was one dish that could never be spoiled by over-long cooking.

If the despatch with which the four of them disposed of it was any criterion, it had certainly not been spoiled! Maman insisted on washing the dishes before she made the coffee that they preferred to the more fashionable tea, and they settled down to a comfortable cose. When Fleur was done with recounting the day's excitement, talk turned to Grandpère's work.

"Have you found your Flora yet?" asked Martine, setting almost invisible stitches into the shirt that she was mending for her husband.

Grandpère scowled. "It is difficult," he admitted. "It seems I shall have to make do with Meg Sturton after all. But it is a sad falling off. It is not even that the part presents any technical difficulty. But Flora is a goddess. For the Flowers it does not signify. If they are earthy, what matter? They are, after all, sprung from the earth. But my Flora should have a spirituelle quality—and that is what I cannot find. *You* could have done it, when you were younger. The child here might have done it, if she had ever been properly taught."

Maman and Fleur exchanged glances—Fleur's mischievous, Maman's amused. "I *was* properly taught, when I was small, Grandpère," offered the girl demurely. "Maman taught me herself."

"To be sure she did," said Grandpère indulgently, "and that is why you hold yourself up properly and move so well. But childhood lessons are not enough, petite. The secret of good style is—"

"Daily practice," chanted two voices in unison.

Grandpère looked slightly affronted. "Precisely what I was about to say," he agreed. "But I cannot see what is so amusing about a plain statement of fact."

"Only that it is exactly what Maman was used to say to me, in just so solemn a voice," explained Fleur, still smiling a little. And then, suddenly serious, "And I did it, too, Maman. It was a kind of spell, you see. Like sticking pins into a wax figurine, only mine was a good spell. If I performed my task faithfully, some day we would meet again. It worked, too, didn't it?"

Martine did not answer at once. The lump in her throat at the picture of a lonely little girl so faithfully doing her exercises and seeking comfort in magic and charms made speech difficult.

"And did you really practise every day? All these years?" asked Papa-Paul—the name that he and Fleur had agreed upon—curiously.

Fleur nodded vehemently. "Truly! It was difficult at school. The bed rail served well enough as a barre, but there was no mirror, so I could not see my mistakes. But I did the best I could."

"Dance for us, then," demanded Grandpère. "This I must see before I will believe."

Fleur jumped up at once. Martine looked anxious, knowing Grandpère's standards and fearful that her darling could never measure up to them.

"There is no room," she protested, "and no music either."

"There is room enough for me to judge her quality," retorted Grandpère, "and as for music, I will play my flute for her. Or Paul, here, shall play his violin."

Paul was already pushing furniture aside to make a space. "What shall it be, child?" asked Grandpère. "A galliard? A pavane?"

"No," said Fleur sharply. "Not a pavane. I—I am not in the mood. Something gay. A jig—a hornpipe."

"A dancer should know no mood save the mood of the music," said Grandpère severely. "However, it shall be as you wish. Listen, then. This is your music."

He played it through for her twice, a merry, lilting gypsy of a tune. She listened attentively, her lips curving to an elusive little smile. She would like to confound Grandpère for Maman's sake, and a little, too, for her husband's, who had liked her dancing. When the tune came to an end she nodded cheerfully. "I have it," she said, and suggested that the two spectators should stand in the doorway to give her more room. "For this is a girl that I saw in the poultry market this morning. You will not be shocked, I beg, for I do not think she was greatly concerned with the behaviour proper to a lady!"

When the music began again she was ready for it, arms akimbo, head tilted in impudent swagger, nose in the air. Before their startled eyes a saucy country

wench expressed her delighted anticipation of the
day's outing, drove her geese to the market, greeted
her friends, chaffered with the customers, flirted
with this one, snubbed another, drooped discon-
solate because her sweetheart had not met her, then
saw him coming in the distance and ran laughing
into his arms.

Since all this display had been aimed at Grandpère, she rather naturally ended up in his arms instead. The precious flute dropped forgotten from
his fingers as he enfolded her in a hug so fierce
that she emerged breathless, declaring that it was
all Maman's fault. Since coming to London, not
once had she done her exercises. And see—one
tiny dance and behold her exhausted!

The laughing protest dropped into a deep well of
silence. Fleur, who had thrown herself into a chair
to recover her breath, looked up enquiringly. No
one said anything. Had they not liked her dancing
after all?

Grandpère, at least, looked cheerful enough.
There was an air of brisk determination about him
as he picked up the ill-used flute, set it aside without even examining it for possible injury, and
brought himself a chair to put beside hers. Maman
was watching him in patent anxiety. Did it matter
so much, then, what he thought of her performance? Papa-Paul's face was the most reassuring.
He was quietly setting the room to rights. Catching
her puzzled eyes, he smiled, made dumb-show of
applause, then shrugged and raised shoulders and

eyebrows to heaven in a 'What happens next?' appeal.

Maman sat down beside Grandpère who was nodding contentedly to himself. Apparently she found this disturbing. She clasped her hands against her breast and said agitatedly, "She cannot *do* it, Papa. You must know that she cannot."

Grandpère chose to misunderstand. "Cannot do it, my dear? Of course she can do it. Oh, she will never reach the heights. The talent is there, the style is excellent—never did I dream you were so good a teacher—but it is simple stuff and she is too old to begin on advanced work. A great pity. However, for my Flora she is perfect. Almost I believe you were prescient when you named her Fleur." He beamed delightedly upon his daughter, though his eyes remained watchful and steady.

Fleur stared at him unbelievingly. Maman said, "You know very well that *that* was not my meaning. The child dances beautifully. So. But what of Lord Blayden, who frequents the Rockstone Club? What of her husband when he returns? Do you imagine that *they* will join in the applause for her performance, however artistically perfect it may be?"

Grandpère shrugged. "They will never know. It is Rockstone's whim that the dancers shall be masked. Oh—just a strip of silk across the eyes and temples. A very good notion it is, too. There is something bewitching about a woman's face with that added touch of mystery. And to some of the coarser types it lends an air of refinement," he added frankly.

Martine seized upon this. "Surely you would not wish your own grandchild to associate with these low types," she urged.

"They are not low types in the sense that you imply. Decent, hard-working girls, all of them. Rockstone made a point of it. It's not a bagnio he's running. Respectability is his stock in trade. Several of my Flowers are married. Rose, for instance, has three children. A little overblown, poor Rose, but she's a good worker, and behind the mask she does well enough. Besides, she needs the money."

Maman was silent. Fleur, who had been listening in amazed disbelief, said timidly. "Do you mean, Grandpère, that you are offering me the part of Flora in your ballet?"

He turned to her eagerly. "That's it, my girl. You'll not find it difficult, I promise you. And though the pay is not very much, it will buy you a few fripperies. Besides—you'll enjoy it. Don't tell me you're not heart and soul in your dancing, for I'd not believe you."

All the years of careful training at Melly's hands said no. Maman herself had spoken of the difficulties that beset the path of a dancer. She knew, in her very bones, that Marcus would not approve. But this was a chance of such an adventure as would never come again, and it was true that she loved to dance. If she were to believe one half of the tales that she had heard about her husband, *he* had had adventure a-plenty. Why should she not have just one, small, perfectly respectable adventure of her own? For with Grandpère to look after her she would be quite safe.

"I think I would like that very much," said Mrs. Marcus Blayden.

TWELVE

MARCUS BLAYDEN landed at Dover at the end of October on the tenth anniversary of Nelson's great sea victory at Trafalgar. It had been a vile crossing. He wondered why anyone should ever choose to go to sea at all, far less endure the hazards of sea *fighting* with that incalculable element of the weather to allow for. God knew, the army was bad enough, but at least the earth did not normally rise up and fight against you.

There were, however, certain incalculables, even in the army, as he had recently discovered to his cost. Such as artillery mules, for instance. It was a kick from one of these misbegotten quadrupeds that had stretched him senseless on the even of Ligny. To have got clear away with his vital information about the concentration of the Army of the North between Maubeuge and Chimay, and then to have been prevented from delivering it to the proper quarters by one cross-grained animal's fit of ill temper was enough to try the patience of a saint. And Marcus was no saint, though he had, he knew, come pretty close to discovering St. Peter's verdict on this important question during the past weeks. The battle must have been fought over and around his unconscious body. It seemed likely, from his injuries, that cavalry had charged over him at some time, but of this he had no recollection. His last clear memory was the theft of the mule which had so amply revenged itself. He had been picked up delirious on the battlefield after lying semi-conscious for hours in drenching rain, and since he was wearing civilian clothes and babbling in French it was no one's especial responsibility to see that he was cared for. The hospitals were already crowded to capacity with far more desperate cases. He had been dumped in a barn with a dozen others, of whom those who were able tended their fellows as best they could. The filthy and overcrowded conditions had led to an outbreak of camp fever—the dreaded typhus. Several had died, but somehow Marcus had struggled back to life and awareness of his surroundings. Convalescence, lacking all civilised amenities, had been a slow and painful business. Nor could he desert his companions in misfortune who had been good to him in his own dire need. It was weeks before he was able to make his way to friends in the neighbourhood who at first failed to recognize the gaunt, bearded scarecrow figure of their erstwhile guest.

A week's rest, with warmth and good food, did much to restore him to something of his former vigour, though when impatience drove him to start preparations for his journey home he found himself, to his fury and disgust, a poor feeble creature. With the ending of the campaign his usefulness in Belgium was at an end. And a glorious part he had played, he thought savagely. The very real risks that he had run, the skill with which he had pieced together his information, counted for nothing. Only success counted. And success, thanks to that accursed mule, had been denied him.

So it was in no very pleasant humour that he stepped ashore from the packet having been obliged to take a week over a journey that he would normally have accomplished in three or four days, and already conscious that he would have to spend the night in Dover before proceeding further if he was to avoid a recurrence of the prostrating headache that still punished over-exertion. The physician called in by his friends had assured him that this malaise would pass with returning health. It was a pity, added this genial gentleman, that the scar left by the mule's animosity had not received professional treatment earlier. But a skilful use of cosmetics and a well-chosen wig would do much to disguise it. To Marcus, who could scarcely remember a moment's ill health, the idea that he must now quack and coddle himself—this was his rendering of the physician's advice, was quite bad enough. The suggestion of cosmetics and a wig was the crowning indignity.

But despite everything it was good to be back in England. Almost insensibly his spirits rose. He began to think of home and of his wife. The harvest would be in by now and the quiet season of the year would permit him to post off to Cumberland without delay. A week or so of idling at Blayden and they would drive south again before winter set in. He reckoned up the days. Tonight in Dover, tomorrow at Dakers; a day in Town—perhaps two, since there were one or two minor matters connected with his recent activities that would have to be cleared up—and then he would be his own master. In view of these damned headaches it might be necessary to take an extra day on the journey north, but he might reasonably count on reaching Blayden within ten days.

He ought to have written to her, of course. But at first he had thought that he would be with her as soon as the letter, and now he decided that it would be delightful to take her by surprise. During the long weeks of sickness and convalescence she had been much in his thoughts. He had only to close his eyes to picture her as she had danced the pavane that last night at Blayden, to conjure up the innocent witchery in her pose as she lifted her head for his approval. He began to wonder if it was really necessary to stay overnight at Dakers. But after so long an absence there were bound to be a dozen things awaiting his decision. Better to deal with them first. Then he could devote his undivided attention to the little bride who had waited so long for his coming.

Two days later he strolled into his rooms at the Albany. It was already dusk—he had been delayed at Dakers even longer than he had reckoned, and Dearden was gone out. This was not surprising, since he had sent no word of his coming. He would stroll round to his club and catch up on the news of the Town, snatch a bite to eat and turn in early. In pursuance of which plan he tossed his valise on to the bed where Dearden could not fail to see it as soon as he came back, decided that his neckcloth would pass muster and was on his way out when his eye fell upon a letter lying on a side table. Recognizing Deborah's writing at a glance, he did not particularly study the superscription but ripped it open eagerly, hungry for news of home. Even as he did so the thought crossed his mind that it was odd that there were no letters from his wife, hitherto so regular a correspondent.

The letter began, 'My dear Sister'. Closer inspection showed that it was addressed, not to him, but to his wife. So Fleur must be in Town. Where was she staying, and what business had brought her there, he wondered. From surprise he passed to delight that the long journey north would be unnecessary. Why, he might even be able to find her this very evening. He contemplated making a round of the more likely hotels, then realised that, almost certainly she would be staying with friends. It would be better to wait until Dearden came back. He would be sure to know all about it.

Unfortunately, Dearden, unaware of the impatience with which his return was awaited, did not come back until eleven o'clock. And when his pleasure in his master's return had been duly expressed, the news that he had to give was not very satisfactory. Yes, certainly Mrs. Blayden had been in London. Presumably she still was, since letters from Blayden came for her almost every week. But Dearden himself had not seen her since the end of July. He did not know where she was staying, and his instructions were to forward letters and messages to her lawyers.

Nothing could be done that night. Marcus was left to ponder the puzzle and make what he could of it. An interview with Mr. Sickling's head clerk next morning proved equally disappointing. Mr. Sickling was ill. He had the influenza and was not expected to be back at his desk for a week at least. In his absence the clerk cound not undertake to furnish the caller with Mrs. Blayden's addrss. He would, of course, send at once to Mr. Sickling, but it would be two days before a reply could be looked for since Mr. Sickling had unfortunately taken ill at his sister's house in Buckinghamshire.

Frustrated and slightly uneasy, Marcus embarked

on a fruitless tour of some of the better known hotels. There was no *reason* for anxiety—it was just
that the whole business seemed so secretive—quite
out of character with the frank and artless child that
he had married. Why was she hiding herself away
behind a lawyer's office? And what was old Pennington about to let her go roaming about the
country in this reckless fashion?

He dined at his club after a singularly irritating
wasted day, but was a little cheered when he was
joined by his friend, Harry Redfern. "Col told me
you was back," said Harry, grinning all over his
pleasantly friendly face. "Never so pleased to hear
anything in my life since the time my old Aunt
Martha left me a handsome legacy that I didn't
expect. Thought you'd cocked up your toes when
there was no word of you after Fleurus. What
happened?"

Marcus's account of his experiences was necessarily brief. It was impossible to be confidential in
the club. There was too much coming and going.
Quite a number of people stopped for a word with
young Blayden, remarking that they had not seen
him for an age. But Harry knew the circumstances
well enough to fill in the bare outlines for himself,
and nodded soberly. It had been, he guessed, a
damned near-run thing.

Presently he said cheerfully, "I suppose you'll be
off to Blayden right away? Damned inconvenient
time for old Pennington to pop off the hooks. Your
wife's going to miss the gayest season that London's

known this century. But I suppose you're too newly wed to care for all the fashionable squeezes."

Another interruption occurred before Marcus could answer. This time he was glad of it. The news of Mr. Pennington's death was something of a shock since he had last seen that gentleman in robust health. And more than ever he wondered what his wife was doing in Town. During the early months of her mourning she would not be able to attend even the quietest of functions without incurring disapproval. Perhaps she had come on business connected with her grandfather's estate. But he really could not imagine so young and feminine a creature knowing anything about business. So, why?

He told Harry, carefully casual, that his plans were not quite certain. He had to see some physician fellow tomorrow. Col had insisted on that—a lot of needless fuss, but that was Col's way—and he seemed to set great store by this particular medico. Then he rather supposed he ought to call on his father before he went out of Town or there would be the devil to pay the next time they met, on the score of filial observances.

"Well that's easy enough," said Harry. "See the old man any time you like. Just take a look-in at Rockstone's. That's his latest haunt. And by the way, he's having the most fantastic run of luck. Never anything like it. If he goes on like this you'll inherit a fortune yet, my lad. Seems he just can't lose, these days. The rankest outsiders—the bones

—it's getting to the stage where he vows it's becoming a dead bore."

The idea of a casual encounter with his parent in a gaming club appealed to Marcus. Until the situation with regard to his wife's presence in Town was a little clearer, he preferred to avoid intimate conversation. In such brief exchanges as were possible in so public a place he need give nothing away, yet might, if he were sufficiently alert, pick up some hint of her present whereabouts.

Their arrival at the club was well timed. A number of the guests were just beginning to drift towards the supper rooms. The tense silence that reigned when play was in progress had given way to a rising hum of conversation. Marcus saw his father almost at once, seated at a table at the far end of the room where play had not yet finished. He crossed over to stand beside him, quietly watching the fall of the cards until the rubber came to an end and the table broke up.

"Whist, sir?" he enquired, raising an amused eyebrow. "Not your usual game, surely?"

His lordship lifted slender fingers to his mouth to conceal a yawn. "You are very right," he said languidly. "A pedestrian affair. But one must do something to counter boredom." He eyed his son thoughtfully. "And you?" he queried gently. "I heard you were back from the Continent. The climate does not seem to have suited your constitution. Far be it from me to interfere, but by the looks of you a period of rural peace might be more beneficial than the racket of Town."

Marcus flushed and stiffened. This solicitude was a new come-out. Prosperity must have exercised a softening influence on his progenitor. "Thank you sir. I shall do very well. A slight touch of fever, now happily past."

Lord Blayden shrugged. "As you will. You will scarcely be socialising in any event, in view of the —er—bereavement in your wife's family. Does she join you in Town, or do you journey to Blayden to fetch her? If that is your plan, you will be well advised to take the journey by easy stages."

So his father knew nothing of Fleur's movements, but supposed her to be still at Blayden. It was strange, to say the least of it, that she could have been in Town for as much as four months without any word of her presence reaching him. He returned an indifferent answer, saying that he rather thought he was fixed in Town for a few days. Lord Blayden went off to join a party of friends who were just leaving, saying over his shoulder, "This place isn't what it was. Too crowded and too noisy by half since they brought in these damned entertainers," and Marcus was left to rejoin Harry.

"May as well have a bite of supper, as we're here," suggested that young man. "Myself, I don't care for gaming above half, but I must say I'd like to run my eye over this dancer there's so much talk about."

It seemed to Marcus as reasonable a way of passing the time as any. He followed his friend to the supper room. It was both crowded and noisy, as his father had said. There could be no doubt that the club was extremely popular with the younger men, whatever the hardened gamesters might think. Harry was heaping a plate from a selection of cold meats temptingly set out on a side table. Marcus, who had dined late, was not hungry but accepted a glass of champagne from a hurrying waiter. He sipped cautiously—the food and wine served at these club suppers were always suspect— but this was quite tolerable and he drank thirstily. Sometimes he thought that he would never forget the torments of thirst that he had endured in his fever. Never again would he take the pleasure of a cool sparkling drink for granted. He lent only half an ear to Harry, who, between bites, was explaining the spectacle that they were about to witness. His mind had gone back to an evening in the library at Blayden. Then, too, he had drunk champagne. He watched the silvery cords of bubbles rising in his glass and, framed between them, pictured a slender figure, regal in mulberry brocade.

A sudden falling away in the babble of voices roused him. Music came pleasantly to his ears and the curtains that had screened the far end of the room were drawn back to reveal a painted pastoral scene. On a softly rounded hillock a young shepherd was playing his pipes beneath the trees. From their shadow there emerged a Being, a creature of verdure and light, drifting effortlessly on slender bare feet. A young girl, clad in floating classical draperies of softest leafy green that hinted at the perfection of ivory limbs beneath. Dark silky hair bounded by a silver fillet streamed about her shoulders and a tiny strip of green silk mask hid the upper part of her face. The Goddess Flora was about to summon her court.

The habitués, the connoisseurs and the curious settled down to their varying enjoyment of the performance. At the other end of the room Marcus Blayden held himself rigid in a blaze of fury that seemed too fierce for a human frame to contain. Despite the trappings of the theatre, despite make-up and mask, the moment that she had begun to dance he had recognised his wife.

THIRTEEN

LATER when he was able to look back at events in more temperate mood, Marcus was to give thanks for the long and stringent training that he had received in the difficult art of maintaining an imperturbable front in the face of imminent discovery. It certainly helped him now. The impulse to rush forward, snatch up his wife from the eyes of that goggling throng, and bear her away to a decent privacy where he could administer the punishment that she so richly deserved, was almost too strong for him. Nor was it consideration for his wife's feelings that held him back, but rather the knowledge of the appalling scandal that such action would precipitate. How dare she, a Blayden, his wife, so expose herself for the entertainment of the gapers? He had no eye at all for the artistry that held a captious audience enchanted, and the tumultuous applause that acknowledged Flora's farewell curtsy was bitter in his ears.

Somehow he managed to subdue the craving for instant action, to listen to Harry's enthusiastic praise. But he was not sorry when his unwonted taciturnity caused his friend to glance at him enquiringly and then give vent to an exclamation of dismay.

"Good God, old fellow! Are you all right? Damned idiot that I am, dragging you out here when anyone with an atom of common sense could have seen at once that you're only fit for your bed. Here!" He summoned a hovering waiter. "Bring me some brandy. And look sharp about it."

Anything in the nature of a scene that would focus public attention on him was the last thing that Marcus wanted, and fury, rather than physical weakness, was responsible for the pallor and the grim-set mouth that had so alarmed his friend, but he was swift to seize upon the excuse so obligingly offered him. Though he assured Harry—with perfect truth—that he was well enough, he permitted himself to be overborne and accepted without complaint an opinion that he looked burnt to the socket. At Harry's insistence he drank the brandy and even obeyed an injunction to button up the collar of his cloak, but the suggestion that a chair should be summoned was going too far.

"Just you *do*, my lad, and it's yourself will be needing it," he warned, in a voice that certainly held no trace of invalidism. "Enough is enough. Very well, I'll go home. I'll even accept your escort so far, since nothing less will satisfy you. But set a curb on your ambitions at that point, dear fellow. Any notions you may be cherishing about putting me to bed with a hot brick to my feet and Dearden standing over me with a bowl of pap, are out. Understood?"

And Harry, delighted that the brandy and the cool evening air had so wonderfully restored his friend, meekly subsided.

It was fortunate that neither he nor Dearden was permitted to witness the display of violence to which the invalid yielded once he had seen the door safe shut behind the reluctant Harry. They would certainly have felt it imperative to summon a physician, if not an attendant from Bedlam! Up and down the floor he prowled, looking like nothing so much as a jungle cat preparing to leap upon its prey. The furnishings of the apartment suffered sadly. A fine Hepplewhite chair which had the misfortune to obstruct his passage was hurled against the wall to the sad detriment of its delicately designed shield back. A luckless china shepherdess, whose silly simper made him think of pastoral ballets, was hurled into the hearth.

The explosive crash of her fall seemed to exercise a soothing effect on her destroyer. The pace of

his prowling slackened and the face of fury gave
way to an expression of fierce concentration. Once
he was sufficiently cool for constructive thought
it did not take him long to reach two firm conclu-
sions. He must have his wife out of that galère
without delay, and the removal must be accomplished with the minimum of fuss and noise. If so
much as a whisper as to her identity were to creep
out, her social ruin would be complete. To his
credit be it said that, although he was still furiously
angry with her, the thought of abandoning her to
her fate never entered his head. He could not
imagine what had persuaded her to embark on such
a crazy prank, but no doubts of her innocence
clouded his firm intent to extricate her from the
scrape into which—and he owned it honestly—his
own neglect had allowed her to tumble.

How could it best be achieved? There were forty-
odd interminable hours to be got through before he
could hope to have news of her whereabouts from
Sickling. In that time the scandal might break and
then it would be too late to save her from the consequences of her folly. He must have speech with
her before then. He set himself to recall those scraps
of Harry's discourse to which he had lent but half
an ear—a discourtesy that he now regretted. Harry
had smiled over John Rockstone's attempt to wrap
his dancers in mystery by masking them. "As
though any patron of the ballet could not name
them all without difficulty after watching them for
a while. The Flora is the only newcomer. No one

seems to have any idea as to *her* identity."

But there were plenty who would devote their energies to discovering it, thought Marcus anxiously. It was just the kind of sport that would have intrigued *him*, and that not so very long ago. He was unashamedly grateful to Providence for Rockstone's notion of having the dancers masked, but one could not rely upon so flimsy a protection. He took what comfort he could from the recollection that Harry, who had met his wife, had certainly not recognised her, despite the admiring gaze with which he had watched her performance.

Eventually he reached the conclusion that his best plan would be to visit the club again. He would stay at the back where she would not see him— for he knew her well enough to guess that she was quite capable of greeting his appearance with such expression of frank delight as must betray them both—and send up his card with an invitation to supper, in the style of an infatuated admirer. He took the added precaution of slipping the card into an envelope and sealing it, so that no interested party should afterwards connect his name with the dancer's disappearance.

When the doctor had done with him next day, informing him in disgusted accents that he had been wasting his—the doctor's—time, for a finer physical specimen he would like to meet, though maybe a little more flesh on his bones would better become him and a week or two of ruralising would not come amiss, he spent the rest of the day in a fever

of impatience. He also spent it in skulking about
Town in a fashion calculated to draw down upon
him the derision of his friends if ever they should
chance to hear of it. Since it was essential that he
go alone to his self-appointed rendezvous, he must
needs avoid all his customary haunts where the
acquisition of a companion was almost unavoidable.
Also it was raining. He could think of only one
place where he was unlikely to meet anyone that
he knew. He spent the afternoon in the British
Museum.

Early evening found him back in his apartment,
with strict instructions to Dearden to inform all
callers that he was gone out of Town, the while he
performed a meticulous toilet. Of set purpose he
came late to the club, strolling quietly into the
supper room when the ballet was half over. Tonight
he was able to appraise his wife's performance in
less hostile mood. Unwillingly he admitted its
charm. The ballet itself was trivial. Setting and
costumes were effective, the dancers were well
trained, the music of pleasant quality, but only the
joyous freshness of the première danseuse lent that
touch of distinction which, as Harry had told him,
was attracting a growing audience. Marcus was
thankful when it was over. The danger of discovery
seemed to him a very real one.

In order to remain inconspicuous he behaved like
any other guest, eating some of the excellent supper
provided and drinking a glass of wine, waiting until
most of the company had settled once more to

their gaming. Then he summoned one of the attendants and handed him the sealed billet, bidding him present it to Madame Flora and ask if she would honour the sender by supping with him.

The waiter pocketed the coin which accompanied the message, bowed his thanks, and bore the envelope away, to be delivered in due course to Mr. Rockstone. That gentleman slit the wrapper, saw that it contained only a card, and did not even trouble himself to glance at it, tossing it into a basket on the floor beside his desk with an accuracy of aim that owed much to recent practice. "Flora?" he enquired. The waiter bowed. "Usual answer," grunted Mr. Rockstone, and returned to his reckoning.

Following his habitual pattern in these circumstances, the waiter allowed a reasonable time to elapse before approaching the sender of the message. His face was carefully composed in an expression of respectful regret, his voice lowered to a confidential tone that could not be overheard by any casual bystander. Like his employer, he had had considerable practice of late.

"Miss Flora wishes me to thank you, sir, for your kind invitation. She appreciates the honour that you do her. But as she has not the pleasure of your acquaintance, her sense of decorum will not permit her to accept."

Over the past weeks the waiter had delivered that message with slight variations when some expensive trifle had been enclosed with the invitation, to quite a number of hopeful gentlemen. It had been received, according to age and temperament, with anything from a rueful shrug to a cynical sneer, but, in general, with a decent complaisance. Never before had the suppliant's face whitened with fury before his very eyes, the mouth hardened into a line about as yielding as a sprung man-trap. The waiter actually backed an anxious pace or two. It looked as though so much pent-up venom might well erupt to his own detriment. But after one or two tense moments the gentleman's heavy lids were lowered to veil the anger in the steel-bright eyes, and the voice which said, "Very well. That is all," sounded coldly indifferent.

Nevertheless the waiter, who was grateful to Miss Flora for the extra pickings that her popularity had brought to his pocket, kept a watchful eye, so far as his duties permitted, on one whom he had no hesitation in describing as an uncommon nasty looking customer. Just the sort of cove that might resort to physical violence to attain his ends, if he chanced to set eyes on the little dancer. But all seemed to be well. To be sure, the gentleman disposed of a bottle of the club's excellent burgundy with rather more speed than was strictly seemly, but he was evidently one who could carry his wine, for then he took his departure without further fuss or complaint. The waiter watched him go and thankfully dismissed the incident from his mind.

Marcus was wrestling with a storm of such violent emotion as he had never known. So the lady had not "the pleasure of his acquaintance," the insolent little jade! Well, *that* could easily be mended, and he would see to it that this time there was no doubt about the matter! All the softer feelings that had grown with him during the long hours of waiting were swept away. To think that he had brought himself to forgive her scandalous behaviour on the score of ignorance and youthful folly! That he had planned as best he knew to protect her from the consequences of that folly; and now she vowed she did not know him!

Very well. She should learn a sharp lesson. But as his resolve hardened and his temper cooled, he remembered that it was still necessary to avoid an open scandal. Anger must not be permitted to betray him into rashness. His plans must be careful and thorough to cover every eventuality. This time there should be no loophole for escape.

FOURTEEN

It took him just over a week to complete his
arrangements. He was helped considerably by the
unsuspected romantic streak in the heart of Mr.
Sickling. Upon receiving his clerk's urgent message,
that gentleman had been much moved by the
thought that there should be any unnecessary delay in the reunion of the married pair. He had
arranged that one of his brother-in-law's grooms
should ride at once for the Albany with a note
explaining that Mrs. Blayden was presently residing
with her Mama, Madame Paul de Trèvy, in Hans
Town.

This helpful missive was awaiting Marcus's re-

turn from the Rockstone Club after that humiliating
snub from his wife, and did much to crystallise his
inchoate ideas into a clear-cut plan of campaign.
He assumed from the outset that his wife's family
would unite to keep her from him if they could.
'Mama' was undoubtedly the Frenchwoman whose
interference Robert Pennington had feared—the
reason for the hurrying on of the marriage. But in
any event he had had his fill of the meddling of
relatives. The matter must now be settled between
his wife and himself. He viewed the prospect with
a certain grim relish.

His preparations took him out of Town on two
occasions, on the second of which he was obliged to
use his father's town coach for the journey, so many
were the packages and bundles to be accommo-
dated. He was also called up to exercise those
talents which had lately been devoted to the service
of his country in the gathering of information. It
was not quite so easy to pass unnoticed in law-
abiding England as it had been in faction-torn
France, especially in so bright and open a neighbourhood as Hans Town, but over the years he
had acquired a certain facility in disguise and a
considerable talent for blending with his background which now stood him in good stead.

In the guise of a Frenchman seeking relatives
missing since the Terror of '93 he acquired a good
deal of information about the little household in
Hans Town. It came as something of a shock to
discover that Madame de Trèvy was, in fact, Ma-

dame la Comtesse de Trèvy, his informant explaining that since the de Trèvy estates had vanished into the maw of the new nobility the de Trèvys preferred to pursue their quiet lives in peaceful England, but it did not deter him from his purpose.

The musical dilettante who invited M. Lavelle to lunch with him at the Clarendon to discuss a series of concerts devoted to the works of Mozart, and the sporting gentleman who began to patronise a small but decent livery stable just off Cadogan Square, bore no resemblance to each other save in the matter of height. The one was precise, slightly effeminate and languid of manner. He laid claim to French descent, a claim supported by his easy use of the French tongue. The other was brisk, bluff and hearty and spoke with a pronounced north country brogue. Each of these gentlemen contributed considerably to Marcus Blayden's knowledge of his wife's movements.

Like most successful strategies his plan was very simple. He had discovered that his wife went to and from the Rockstone Club each evening escorted by her grandfather in a carriage hired for the purpose from the livery stable near Cadogan Square. This practice had gone on perfectlly smoothly for weeks —had, in fact, become established routine. It seemed very probable that, if Grandpapa's presence should be suddenly and urgently required elsewhere —say, perhaps to meet some renowned instrumentalist, just the man for the projected concerts, who chanced to be passing through London—that

Grandpapa would see no cause for alarm and would not hesitate, for once, to consign his charge to the care of the driver. The driver was easy. If he would not yield his place to bribery he would yield to physical force.

Once or twice, during the course of that very busy week, Marcus found time to wonder what his wife was making of the silence that had followed her refusal to see him. Surely she could not imagine that he would tamely submit to such treatment? If she did, she would soon discover her mistake! He had half expected her to write to him, explaining that some unknown difficulty had prevented her from acceding to his request and arranging a rendezvous. But day succeeded day without a word. He hardened his heart.

His plans worked even more smoothly than he had anticipated, for on the appointed night he was favoured by the weather. M. Lavelle had accepted his new acquaintance's imperative summons to a very late supper, rather crossly because, as he said, he was getting too old for late nights, but with no suspicion that he was being neatly got out of the way. Since the invitation—if one could so describe it—had only reached him while the ballet was actually in progress, it was too late to make alternative arrangements for Fleur's escort. He did not worry unduly. The distance was quite short, the driver had always been sober and reliable. He escorted his grand-daughter to the waiting carriage without a qualm. Since heavy rain was falling it was only natural that the driver should have his coat collar turned up and his hat pulled well down. M. Lavelle handed Fleur into the shabby familiar vehicle, repeated an injunction that no one was to wait up for him, and hurried back to the shelter of the vestibule as the carriage moved off.

Fleur, a little tired after the evening's performance, curled down in her corner, watched for a while the dazzle of occasional lights through the driving rain, and presently fell asleep. She roused when the carriage stopped, assuming that they had reached home, opened the door and scrambled down, still only half awake, before she realised her mistake.

The carriage had pulled up inside a vast coach house, dimly lit by two stable lanterns. Her driver had already swung down from his seat and was unharnessing the jaded old horse with swift competence. Close at hand stood a neat chariot with two good-looking chestnuts already harnessed up. The groom at their heads glanced across incuriously at the new arrivals, then turned away as though they were no concern of his.

Still dazed from sleep and the surprise of her awakening, Fleur swung back towards the driver who had completed his task and now came towards her with leisurely strides, tossing aside his soaked beaver and stripping off the shabby driving coat as he came. With a stab of pure terror she saw that he was masked, and realisation of her dire peril came with stunning force. She was not granted time for so much as one cry for help. Even as she drew breath for it the man swooped and caught her in his arms, one hand across her mouth.

"No use to cry out, my pretty one," he said, in a nasal whine. "Besides, this is a respectable place. A nobleman's house, no less. They wouldn't like it. As for Job, there," he jerked his head towards the stolid groom, "he's stone deaf. Not that he would listen to you, even if he could hear you. We have but stopped for a change of horses—*and* carriage! You've a little further to travel tonight than just to Hans Town. So in with you, and we'll be off."

He released his hold of her, opening the door of the chariot and sweeping her a travesty of a bow as he stood back for her to enter. She strove to master the fear that seemed to paralyse even her voice and said breathlessly. "You are making a mistake. I have no money. See—here is my purse." She pulled it out and proffered it. "There are but a few guineas left, but it is all I have. Pray take them and let me go. I will not tell anyone, I promise."

The man laughed. A soft, low laugh that sounded a note of pure cruelty in Fleur's frightened ears. "No money?" he asked amusedly. "The wealthy Miss Pennington? Come, my dear, I am not quite the fool you take me for. Put up your purse. It does not interest me. But time presses. So—" and once again he indicated that she should get into the chariot.

At that she panicked and tried to run, an attempt foredoomed to failure. The highwayman—for so she judged him—caught her easily enough and carried her to the chariot. She fought him with all her strength, and for a girl she was both strong and supple, thanks to her love of riding and the years of patient exercise. But twist and turn as she might, there was no evading those prisoning arms that held her so easily, so impersonally, while she wore herself out against their inflexibility and was forced into exhausted submission. A glance at the mouth below the mask showed it smiling still. The frantic, butterfly struggle had amused him.

He tossed her up into the chariot with casual ease, made some sign to the groom, and climbed in beside her. "I don't usually entrust my horses to other hands," he told her, "but it seems that you are not yet convinced that you are wholly in my power. It would be a pity if you were to injure yourself in some foolish attempt at escape. Where, then, would my profit be?"

There was a crumb of comfort in that. If his object was ransom she could banish the far more hideous fear that had been growing within her since she had struggled in vain against the strength of his arms. But the moment of relief was all too short. "I could have tied you up, of course," mused that smooth, hateful voice in the darkness. "But what a pity that would have been. Those pretty wrists should never be bruised by bonds. Only kisses should ever stop those soft lips."

He heard her catch her breath in a frightened little sob, and felt the first stirrings of penitence. He

was behaving very badly, he knew. To be sure she
had deserved punishment, but that last veiled
threat was really carrying things too far. Truth to
tell, he had half expected her to recognise him
despite the mask and his assumed manner, not
making allowances for shock and fear and the complete unexpectedness of his presence. A little
ashamed that he had frightened her more than he
had intended, he fell silent.

Beside him Fleur crouched in a daze of exhaustion and terror. When he made no further remark
after that last sally, nor attempted to touch her, she
plucked up heart a little. Perhaps, after all, the
words were just an ignorant man's mistaken notion
of gallantry, intended to flatter but not to be taken
seriously. Better not to refine too much on them.

On and on they went. Out of Town now, the
paved streets left behind. She wondered where they
were taking her. Despite the darkness and the rain,
they were travelling fast. The road must be very
familiar to the man on the box, the whole business
carefully planned, since the leader had seemed to
know so much about her. But what would they do
when they discovered that she had been speaking
the truth when she said that she had no money—
that there was no hope of ransom? She shivered.
And once begun could not stop. She was wearing
only a thin dress, the shawl that she had wrapped
about her shoulders on leaving the club having
fallen away in her struggles for freedom and been
left behind. As reaction took over, her whole body

was racked by uncontrollable shudders. Despising herself for yielding to what must be construed as a sign of fear, she strove valiantly to hold herself still, but it was useless. Her whole body was shaking with a nervous chill, her teeth chattering audibly.

The man beside her turned his head sharply. "What is it?" he demanded brusquely. "Are you ill?"

She was trembling too violently to answer coherently. "I c-c-can't—" she tried, but the words would not come. He put out a hand to touch hers and swore beneath his breath at its clammy coldness.

"Damnation," she heard him mutter. "And I did not think to bring a rug."

Then he was struggling out of his coat and wrapping it round her shaking body. There was a flask of brandy in one of the pockets of the chariot. He poured a generous measure into the flask top and obliged her to drink it, tilting it down her throat despite her feeble efforts at resistance. Clumsily, in the darkness, he buttoned the coat about her and then pulled her into his arms. At that she began to struggle again, but he only pulled her closer, saying harshly, "Lie still, little fool. I'm only trying to keep some warmth in you. We've an hour to go yet, and after all the trouble you've put me to I don't want you sick of a lung fever."

The potent spirit was already having its effect. The words, for all their surface roughness, were somehow reassuring. Fleur's struggles ceased and

she lay quiescent, a slow, comforting warmth gradually stealing over her. Afterwards she was to wonder
if she had not actually fallen asleep in his arms.
Certainly it did not seem very long before the speed
slackened as the chariot turned sharply into a nar-
row drive.

"Only a few minutes more," said her abductor.
"For the sake of your own dignity let me warn
you that it is no use appealing to the servants. Job,
as you know, is deaf. The others who will wait
on you hear well enough but they are wholly devoted to my service."

"And will no doubt expect their share of the
profits," she said scornfully.

She heard him chuckle softly in the darkness.
"Oh ho! So you've an edge to your tongue, have
you? Good. I've no use for miserable whining
women. And here we are," he added, as the chariot
stopped in front of a sturdy stone-built porch.

Obviously they were expected, for a lamp hanging from the porch roof was alight and even as the
horses checked the door was opened to reveal a
stone-flagged hall with a fine oak staircase leading
from it. A cheerful fire was burning on an open
hearth and a door at the other end of the hall stood
ajar to reveal a small square parlour where a table
was laid ready for a meal.

It seemed an oddly civilised setting for a highwayman, but Fleur was too apprehensive to pay much
attention to her surroundings. She stood silently by
while her captor exchanged a few swift words with

the man who had opened the door, a small shrivelled up little fellow who had but one arm, the left one having been taken off at the elbow, and a pair of blue eyes of an engaging honesty that seemed sadly misleading under the circumstances.

"I trust that you will find everything for your comfort in your room," said the highwayman smoothly. "May I suggest that you exchange that thin gown for something a little warmer? Supper will be ready in half an hour. I daresay you are exceedingly hungry since you will scarcely have eaten before your performance." His teeth gritted slightly on the last word, otherwise his manner was that of a courteous host. She looked at him curiously. In buckskins, riding boots and shirt sleeves— for she was still wearing his jacket—he loomed frighteningly tall, and there was menace, she thought, in the glitter of the eyes behind the mask. She wondered if he retained it to prevent her from identifying him at some future date, then pulled herself up sharply. Never mind the future. It was the urgent present that she had to deal with.

"I thank you, sir, but I am not hungry. With your permission I would prefer to retire at once."

He grinned. "But you do not have my permission. You and I have a good deal to say to one another. It is a sad pity, of course, that we have not been formally introduced, but tonight you shall sup with me whether you will or no. I will brook no refusal. As for retiring—" he broke off, since still she did not recognise him, had not picked up the gauge of his last remark. "We shall see," he said enigmatically. "Meanwhile, here is Elly, to show up to your room and to wait on you."

There was no choice but to obey. With all the dignity that she could summon she walked steadily to the foot of the staircase where the girl—she was little more than a child—awaited her. "Mrs. Melby has put you in the Yellow Room, ma'am," she said, smiling shyly, and led the way up the first flight of stairs to a comfortably furnished chamber where all the necessities of a lady's toilet were already laid out and a pleasant fire glowed a welcome to the weary traveller.

This was becoming more and more dream-like— or nightmare-like—thought Fleur desperately, as she submitted to the girl's diffident ministrations. She had read in forbidden novels, as what schoolgirl had not, of villainous abductors who carried off innocent maids. The maids were always rescued on the brink of disaster by some impossibly perfect hero and the villains came to various unpleasant ends. But none of the stories had prepared her for anything like this. Here was no mysterious castle peopled by sinister retainers, no mouldering dungeon with eldritch hag as jailer. Every outward circumstance insisted that she was a cherished guest to be treated with consideration. Only her mind insisted that she was, in fact, a helpless prisoner. And in her case, alas, there was no hero to come to the rescue even if anyone knew of her plight. When Elly, beaming delightedly, threw open the door of the big clothes press that filled half of one wall and invited her to say which gown she would wear, fear raised its ugly head again. For the press held every kind of gown that a girl could possibly want. There was even, she noticed, a riding habit. And all of them had been most admirably chosen to set off a dark-haired girl of slender build.

Fleur stared at them with dilated eyes, her heart thudding painfully as she realised the implications of these elaborate preparations. But her own dress had been torn in her struggles and, moreover, smelt most unpleasantly of the brandy that had been spilled on it when he forced her to drink. She chose, reluctantly, a dinner dress of cream velvet, because it buttoned high to the throat and the long, close-fitting sleeves would hide the bruises that already showed blue on her arms and shoulders.

Elly brushed out her hair for her but had no skill in dressing it. She proffered a cream velvet snood with cauls of golden net, obviously designed to go with the gown that Fleur had chosen. It was unusual, but easy to slip on. The shining masses of hair were simply coiled up and bundled into the cauls. Then she was ready—and must face whatever ordeal awaited her downstairs.

Her host, if she might call him, had also changed his dress for formal evening clothes but was still masked. In the light of the parlour candles she saw him clearly for the first time and was immediately aware of a teasing resemblance to someone she had seen before. One of her 'admirers' from the club?

Several gentlemen had been extremely pressing in their attentions, which was why she now declined all communication with them. But she could not recall anyone who bore a disfiguring scar—a scar that ran from jaw to temple where the dark hair had been brushed forward to conceal it. He rose courteously at her timid entrance and she allowed him to seat her at the table and enquire her choice among the several dishes. A childish rebellion over such minor matters would in no way serve her cause. Better to submit and save her strength for time of need. The maidservant who waited on them was deft and pleasant and seemed to regard the serving of supper to a masked master at two o'clock in the morning as nothing out of the common way. Fleur guessed he had spoken no more than the truth when he had warned her that it would be useless to appeal to the servants.

She had no idea what she ate though she had, in fact, been faint with hunger. The hot food revived her courage, even though the sense of unreality continued to oppress her. While the maid was in the room they spoke only trivialities. He asked if she had found everything that she required in her room, directed the girl to set a screen to shield her from a possible draught, seemed in all respects perfectly at ease, the courteous, well-bred host. But Fleur found the role of complaisant guest too much for her. Her replies were brief to the point of rudeness, and when she had eaten sufficient to blunt the edge of a hunger that was but natural to a healthy young creature whose last meal had been a light luncheon, her appetite suddenly failed and she found it impossible to choke down another mouthful. The eyes behind the mask were watching her closely but he made no comment, only turning to the maid and dismissing her with a pleasant smile, saying, "That will be all, Anna. I expect your father has remembered to set wine for us in the book-room as I desired him."

As the door closed behind the girl, Fleur rose. "I will bid you goodnight, sir," she said, with a gallant attempt at composure. "I am very tired. And I do not care for wine."

"No?" The voice was coolly amused. "Your tastes have changed, my dear, along with your way of life. You liked it well enough in the library at Blayden. Tonight you will drink it to please me. I do not care for that sober Puritan face, Madame Flora. A wench who can disport herself in public for the amusement of the gapers should know better how to entertain her husband."

One hand had grasped her arm as she shrank back at his first words, the other had gone up to remove the mask. Even without it, Fleur scarcely recognized him. That he was thinner, scarred, was but a part of it. She had never before seen him in a black rage—the rage that still convulsed him at the thought of his wife—*his*—displaying the perfection of her body in public for the delectation of any lecher or pimp who cared to pay down his blunt. That Flora had been the most modest of

goddesses, revealing only a hint of a delicate angle
or beautifully moulded arm beneath her leaf-green
draperies, made no difference to the depth of his
loathing. When he thought of that gloating, grinning audience—for so he pictured them—there was
something akin to murder in his heart.

For Fleur the revelation of his identity came as
the climax to a night of intolerable nervous strain.
The surge of joy that flooded her whole being at the
sight of him was stricken by the bitter disgust, the
savage anger manifest in face and words. She longed
to pour out her delight and her thankfulness, yet
was afraid to do so. And out of the tumble of feelings that sought for expression, the phrase that
found utterance was perhaps the most unfortunate
that she could have chosen.

"Marc!" she faltered. "What *have* you done to
your face?"

Marcus was no vainer than the next man, but
his mirror, let alone the Belgian physician's well-
meant advice, had shown him that the livid scar
of his wound did nothing at all to enhance his appearance. He would not, he felt, have minded so
much if the wound had been taken in battle. Honourable scars were one thing. It was harder to
reconcile oneself to a disfigurement caused by a
stupid and slightly ridiculous accident.

His voice was remote. "A pity, is it not? Small
wonder if you repent of your bargain. Shall I
resume the mask, lest you take me in even greater
disgust? But no—I think not. Masks are for cheats

and deceivers, are they not, my dear? And you and I have both put off ours, and must e'en make the best of what lies behind them."

She stared back at him dumbly, her eyes great pools of pain. So this was the end of her innocent dreams, her tremulous hopes. He hated her—despised her. Oh! Why had she not paid heed to Maman's doubts and warnings? Now he would never forgive her, though indeed she had thought no harm. She turned away to hide the tears that burned in her eyes.

He said harshly, "Of no avail to turn your back on it, my girl. You will grow accustomed in time. And that you shall have in plenty. I have brought you here so that you may learn the conduct becoming to a Blayden and the duties of a wife. For we are done with play acting at marriage. I daresay in time we shall go on as prosperously as most married couples. Once you have learned your lessons we need not see a great deal of each other."

She cried out at that, for it seemed to her the worst thing he had said yet. "Then why did you not leave me where at least I was content? You do not want me. You do not love me."

He laughed; a bitter, unamused little sound. "Love? A sentimental folly for poets and dreamers. And I am neither. I respect certain qualities that I find in you—dignity—courage. Good sense, too, since you did not fall into hysterics despite the anxiety you must have suffered tonight. I am sorry for that," he added on a kindlier note, "and willing to believe that your reckless folly in appearing at that infernal club was largely the result of ignorance and lack of guidance. But when you refused to see me, you left me no choice. How would it have been if my father had chanced to recognise you there?"

For a moment she was puzzled. Then, with a flash of comprehension, she realised what must have happened. Some message from Marc must have been tossed aside among the dozen or so notes that were sent to her daily. That explained a good deal, not least his anger. But this was no time to be stammering excuses. In her own way Fleur was every bit as proud as any Blayden of them all.

"I doubt if Lord Blayden would recognise me if I walked smash into him at Allmack's," she said quietly. "A poor little dab of a female with neither looks nor pedigree to recommend her! And you, for your part, could at least have left me alone—as you did when you married me. *That* choice was still open to you."

"When I married you, you were little more than a child. And I left you in safe keeping," he retorted. "Do you think that I would permit my wife to earn her own living? And as a dancer of all things! You cannot be aware of the reputation that such wenches bear!"

She shrank a little at that but held her head high. "Then you may divorce me," she said fiercely, "since I am not fit to be your wife."

His grim mouth relaxed at that, the hard grey

eyes crinkled in genuine amusement. "We Blaydens may be steeped in several kinds of infany but we do not divorce our wives. Particularly when they are too green and too foolish to be thrown unprotected upon the world. No. Resign yourself, my dear. You *are* my wife and there can be no going back. Remains only to teach you a proper submission."

He took her hands and drew her towards him. She yielded unwillingly but made no attempt at a resistance that she already knew to be useless. The strong fingers that could be so brutal were gentle enough as they caressed her throat and tilted her face to his, deft and quick as they unfastened the buttons that closed the neck of the cream gown. He stooped and set his lips to that wildly fluttering pulse-beat in the slim throat.

"Many times these past months have I wished to do just that," he said thoughtfully. "It is hard on you, my dear, that you must surrender to a scarred caricature of a man, but alas, there is no help for it. For my part I am well enough pleased with my bargain. You are lovely enough to set any man's pulses racing." The deep voice was velvet soft now, as he gathered her closer. "Tonight I think we will dispense with Elly's services. I trust that you will find me an adequate substitute."

FIFTEEN

It was very late next day when Fleur awoke to find herself alone in the big four-poster. The door into the adjoining dressing-room stood wide open but the room was unoccupied. Someone had drawn back the curtains and lit the fire, all so quietly that she had never roused. Pale sunlight was streaming into the room, gilding the yellow hangings that gave it its name. She lay still, staring about her wide-eyed, recalling all the strange events of yesterday until she came to the moment at which Marc had set a firm arm about her waist and brought her to this room.

At this point in her recollections she rolled over

in the big bed and snuggled down like a sleepy kitten, pulling the covers over her head. Not even the gentle sunlight should intrude on that remembered rapture. She had never dreamed that it would be like that. She had known—oh! ages ago, even before they were married—that the mere touch of his hand could set her in a glow; and once, in the library at Blayden, when he had kissed her, she had felt the strangest longing to cling to him and return his kisses with an enjoyment that she vaguely felt to be most improper. But those experiences, pleasant though they had been, had given little indication of the ecstasy to which his love making had awakened her.

She was, blessedly, too innocent to realise that he had used all the arts of an accomplished lover to coax her into willing surrender. He had been very patient, gentling her out of her shyness, her fears, until his caresses had aroused in her a passionate response that had startled him. He had not thought that a maid—and so young and untried a maid— was capable of so generous giving. Afterwards he had cradled her close in his arms, heavy with sleep as she was, and kissed her very gently, a trifle ashamed of his behaviour but exceedingly content with the results.

Remembering his kindness, his tenderness, Fleur hugged herself under the bedclothes. Surely he could not really hate her so much as it had seemed when he had spoken to her so cruelly? Perhaps in time he would forget how badly she had behaved.

As for that perfectly horrid threat about not needing to see very much of each other once she had learned her lessons—she sat up in bed, eyes very solemn at this shocking thought. Then her mouth curved to a demure little smile. How *very* slow she would be at learning them!

Presently she got out of bed and pottered about, exploring the room. She guessed that she was at Dakers, remembering the name because she had thought it a strange one, and longed to set out on a wider exploration but was a little diffident about her next move. She was not quite sure of her standing this morning—whether she was honoured wife or sullen captive. She stole across to the bedroom door and gently turned the handle. As she had half suspected, she was locked in. Well, really! After last night! How could he imagine that she would want to run away?

Indignation gave her sufficient courage to pull the bell. If she was to be treated as a prisoner they should at least feed her—and she was, she discovered, quite amazingly hungry! She pulled a negligée over her nightdress—with a passing thought that the garments that Marc had selected for his wife were *far* more improper than those worn by the Goddess Flora—and scampered back into bed, pulling the quilt up to her shoulders before she could feel herself decently covered.

Elly answered the summons of the bell, bringing hot water and enquiring her mistress's wishes in the way of breakfast. The master had been out

betimes as was his custom but had left orders that
Mrs. Blayden was not to be wakened and was to
stay in bed until he came back as she was quite
worn out by yesterday's journey and their belated
arrival. Fleur eyed that innocent-looking rosy face
with deep suspicion. The girl *must* know that she
had been locked in, since only by unlocking the
door could she have gained admission. To be sure,
Marc had said that the staff were devoted to him,
but did they really accept his locking his wife in
her room as right and proper? Better to make no
protest at the moment. She did not want to make
herself look foolish by issuing orders that the girl
either could not or would not obey. But she would
have something to say to Mr. Blayden when he
chose to put in an appearance.

Unfortunately, after eating an enormous and
quite delectable breakfast, bathing—with an interested appraisal of the progress of her bruises,
and putting on an even prettier nightgown, she fell fast
asleep once more. Thus proving that she had
already learned her first lesson—that husbands always know what is best for their wives—and only
awakening when that gentleman appeared in person
and swept her into a comprehensive embrace that
left her neither breath nor opportunity for the lec-
ture she had meant to read him.

This pleasant interlude over, however, he grew
serious. "If you tried your bedroom door this morning, you found it locked," he said directly.

She nodded, a hint of rebellion in the set of her lips.

"Very well. You have a choice. You may remain a prisoner locked in whenever I am obliged to leave you, since I will not let you out of my keeping again. It will be dull for you, I fear, though I will do my best to make your captivity a comfortable one and will keep you well supplied with books and sewing materials or whatever you choose to occupy yourself with. On the other hand——" he paused and studied her closely for an appreciable time——"if you choose to pledge me your word not to run away, you may emerge from your seclusion and take your proper place as my wife and the mistress of my home."

It was on the tip of Fleur's impulsive tongue to tell him her true feelings on the subject of running away. But despite this morning's hopeful reverie she was still just a little afraid. If he was too sure of her, might he not fulfil his threat of going about his own affairs and seeing as little of his wife as convention permitted? She hesitated, decided hastily on a middle course since the thought of being locked in was unbearable, and said meekly, "I will promise not to run away."

He had not missed that brief hesitation. His brows drew together in swift suspicion. But in their earlier dealings together he had never found cause to doubt her word. And he would be watchful. If she was planning to deceive him she would not find it easy.

"Very well, then," he said lightly. "Up you get, slug-a-bed. And after luncheon I will introduce you to your new domain. Shall I ring for Elly, or—" with a wicked twinkle—"do you prefer *my* services?"

"You may ring for Elly, thank you," said his wife with dignity.

"A wise choice," he conceded ruefully. She looked very sweet and lovable sitting up in the big bed, trying to look very much married and dignified in that absurd but extremely attractive garment that he had chosen for her. If he yielded to the impulse to kiss her again, it was little enough of her new domain that they were like to see beyond the confines of the Yellow Room. Obediently he rang the bell, briskly bade his wife make haste with her dressing, and went downstairs.

Fleur was not the only one with lessons to learn. With a naïveté surprising in one who reckoned himself very much a cynic and man of the world, Marc came gradually to the conclusion that marriage was very different from casual affairs with females of easy virtue. You could no longer keep your life in neatly separated compartments. A wife was there all the time. She had a right to share in your interests and your problems. She was not just a toy that you could, so to speak, put away in a cupboard when you had tired of playing with her. He was surprised to find himself accepting this community of interests with no small degree of pleasure.

He had always enjoyed the part of his life that

was spent at Dakers, but it had been the enjoyment of congenial work, satisfying but solitary. When darkness fell there had been nothing much to do except pore over his accounts or read a book. There was no one to rejoice with him that five of the six calves born that spring were sturdy young heifers, or to sympathise when an unseasonable frost blighted the cherry blossom. Now all that was changed. Fleur was vividly interested in everything connected with the house and the farm. She was ignorant, of course, but it was a pleasure to explain the science of husbandry to so eager and apt a pupil.

Nor did it take her very long to bring the indoor servants round her thumb. And in this instance her success owed nothing to artifice. It must be admitted that, while her love for horses had easily been extended to a genuine interest in the other farm animals, her desire to know more about crop rotation and stall feeding was deliberately cultivated in order to please a husband who liked to talk of such matters. But her enjoyment of housekeeping was frank and honest, her growing affection for Marcus's staff, sincere.

It was very much a family affair, she learned. The one-armed butler and the cook-housekeeper were husband and wife; Anna and Elly, the maids she had met that first night, were their daughters. She took her first step in their esteem quite unwittingly when she declined Marcus's offer to hire a properly trained dresser for her, since Elly was but fourteen and quite untaught. Truth to tell, she disliked the

notion of some superior town-bred damsel intruding
on her private paradise with inquisitive eyes and
gossiping tongue, and despising their homely way
of living. Elly was both loyal and discreet, said
Fleur, remembering that locked bedroom door. She
was perfectly capable of keeping her mistress's
belongings in good order, hooking up her gowns
and laundering that fragile muslin or sinken underwear that still made its owner blush at her own re-
flection when she chanced to catch sight of it. If
she could not dress hair in the latest fashion, what
did that matter, here in the country? Especially,
she might have added, when one had a husband
who took a wicked delight in filching one's hairpins,
calmly announcing that he liked best to see her hair
loose, and why should the patrons of the Rockstone
Club be permitted a privilege that was denied to
him?

Mrs. Melby was the last to capitulate, perhaps
because she spent most of her time in the kitchen
and so saw least of the married pair. Also because,
if the whole family was devoted to the master, Mrs.
Melby idolised him. Who else, she demanded,
would have employed a one-armed butler, even if
the arm *had* been lost in his country's service, just
because years and years ago a young lass just start-
ing work in his mother's kitchens had set her heart
on marrying Jim Melby, when he had two arms
just as good as anyone else's before the press gang
took him? Mrs. Melby didn't see how an independent chit of a girl who had to be kidnapped and

then locked up in case she ran away could possibly be worthy of her adored master. Fleur's first reception in the kitchen was very stiff.

The atmosphere mellowed a little when the girl said how much she had enjoyed her breakfast and hoped, shyly, that her lateness had not entirely disrupted the kitchen routine. There could be no doubting the sincerity of the young lady's compliments, especially when one had seen the well-polished plates that had come down on the breakfast tray. Mrs. Melby unbent sufficiently to speak of the difficulty of tempting the master's appetite since his illness. Not near enough did he eat for a man of his inches and now so thin as he was since that dreadful fever. She realised that she was holding her listener spellbound.

She reported the conversation that followed to her assembled family when the day's work was done. "Looked at me with eyes like great black inkpots, she did, and her face as white as flour. 'I didn't know, Mrs. Melby,' she says. 'He did not tell me. But I ought to have guessed for myself, seeing him so changed.' And then she asks me what she ought to do, almost as if I'd been her own Ma. Downright concerned she was, and that I *will* say."

"And what did you tell her, Ma?" enquired Anna with deep interest.

Mrs. Melby bridled. "I told her to make him laugh," she announced triumphantly. "Feeding him she can leave to me and well able I am to do it, though I *do* say so myself. But there's nothing like a good hearty laugh for giving a man an appetite for his victuals and helping to put the flesh on his bones."

Her family regarded her with startled respect, but after some animated discussion with several graphic examples drawn from personal acquaintance, it was generally conceded that there might well be something in what she said.

By the end of the first week Mrs. Melby was prepared to admit that the master could have done worse. "A great heiress she is, by all accounts, but there's no finicking nonsense about her and she's not too proud to put her hand to any job that needs doing. Came and helped me stone the raisins this morning while she was talking about opening up the rooms that's not been used since old Sir Caspar died. 'I'm remembering what you said, Mrs. Melby,' she whispers, when he comes shouting for her to go and look at something or other. Maybe after all she'll suit him better than I thought."

Whether Fleur did indeed try to follow Mrs. Melby's advice or whether returning health was working its own miracle, Marcus was certainly less grim and gaunt looking and his laughter was heard almost often enough to satisfy his devotee. Deliberately or not, his wife amused him. Even when, as frequently happened, they disagreed. No arguments of his would persuade her that she had been wrong to accept Grandpère's offer. She was sorry that she had angered him, but in her own view she had done nothing wrong—certainly nothing disgraceful. Her husband now knew all the circumstances—all about Mr. Pennington's will and the needy little family in Hans Town. The dancing had been something she could do to help them, and she had done it. She was honest enough to admit that she had thought it would be an adventure and also that the novelty had very soon palled, the repeated performances grown wearisome. But when a girl had only fifteen pounds a year, she must do as best she could.

This unexpected toughness of moral fibre first exasperated him and then earned his reluctant respect. It was all the more surprising because her physical capitulation was complete. In his arms she was all tenderness, all melting submission. But that did not mean, apparently, that she inevitably regarded his judgments as superior, his word as law. When he pointed out that, whatever the hardship inflicted by Mr. Pennington's will, she had been amply provided for as long as she remained at Blayden, she said only, "But what about Maman and my little brother? Besides, you had given me no reason to suppose that you were sincerely attached to me. When your letters stopped coming how was I to know that you had not deserted me?"

Instinct, and a growing understanding of the man she had married, warned her that pretty coaxing ways would not serve with Marcus. Perhaps her knowledge of his past suggested that he would have had a considerable experience of such feminine

wiles, designed to wheedle a jewel or a handsome
present from him. He was much more susceptible to
reasoned argument. Whether her resistance teased
or merely amused him, his respect for her integrity
grew with every such encounter. In self defence he
told her a little of his story. She listened in silence
to a vague but roughly truthful account of meeting
with a slight accident and then being caught up
in the aftermath of battle; then said pertinently,
"But what were you doing in Fleurus in the first
place—right in the path of the French advance—
when you were supposed to be in Brussels? And
what sort of an accident?"

He did not want her enquiring too closely into
the nature of his work in Belgium. To distract her
he tried to fob her off with a mildly humorous version of his encounter with the mule. His friends had
seemed to find it highly diverting. Not so his wife.
But neither did she express wifely concern or
sympathy.

"There, now!" said Mrs. Blayden crossly. "I
always *did* think that mules were one of God's
mistakes. What's more, I'm persuaded that He
thought so, too, and that's why he made them in-
fertile. But of course clever people must know
better than God and went on breeding them. And
now just see what has come of it!"

She sounded so indignant about it that Marcus
shouted with laughter and ended by catching her in
his arms and kissing her soundly. And for the first

time Fleur ventured to put up a timid hand and touch the scar with gentle fingers and assure him that it was fading fast.

SIXTEEN

DAY succeeded day, and with each one Fleur's hopes for a happy future grew more confident. To be sure, Marc rarely made her pretty speeches, and his endearments—if one might so describe them—were unusual. He was more apt to address her as 'woman' or 'wench' or even 'impudent brat' than to employ the tender terms that she had always understood to be the common currency of lovers. But what need of those when his actions so plainly proclaimed his thought for her?

Whenever it was possible he took her with him, riding or walking about the estate and the neighbouring countryside. If the day's task was too heavy

or too dirty for a girl to share, or the weather too
rough, he was careful to enquire if she had sufficient
to occupy and interest her within doors. As he grew
to trust her more fully, he would ask if she would
not like Job to drive her into Rochester, where
there were some excellent shops. Often, when he
came home on days such as these, he would have
some small treasure to show her—a cunningly
woven wren's nest—a spray of gaudy autumn-tinted
leaves—a branch of scarlet-berried holly; and once,
buttoned inside his jacket, a half-starved kitten
that he had found, caught but uninjured in a rabbit
snare. Only once had he left her for a whole day
when he had gone up to Town on business. He had
not invited her to go with him and she had not
liked to suggest it, though she would dearly have
loved to pay a visit to Hans Town and need not
have interfered with his engagements. It had seemed
a very long day. Nor had he said anything about his
activities when he did at last return, but since
Grandpapa Pennington had never discussed business affairs either, she did not find this surprising.

She did not doubt that she was much in his
thoughts. She knew that he found her desirable.
Almost she was convinced that he loved her. But
one circumstance still puzzled and disturbed her.
Each day, usually very early in the morning, he
would disappear, for as much as two or three hours.
She had not quite reached the point of asking him
outright where he went on these occasions, but
curiosity was growing to a painful intensity within

her, and, alas! jealousy, too. She could never quite forget the tales that had been told of him. Even Melly, in distant Cumberland, had heard of his shocking reputation. Maman and Papa-Paul had endorsed the stories. And Rose, kind, motherly, hard-working Rose, speaking in scathing comment on Lord Blayden and not knowing that her remarks were addressed to that gentleman's daughter-in-law, had innocently remarked how different a one was his son. An acquaintance of hers had once enjoyed Mr. Blayden's protection for a few weeks and had held him in affection ever since. Fleur had known from the outset that her husband was no Galahad. How if the time that he spent away from her was passed in the arms of some light o' love? She was very young, deep in love, and abysmally ignorant of such affairs. It never entered her head that six o'clock on a cold December morning was a very queer time to be leaving one's warm bed and one's distinctly attractive wife to go visiting a mistress.

There came a day when he went out even earlier than usual, leaving the house long before she woke. Anna told her that he had gone to see one of the horses, but when she visited the stables after breakfast there was no sign of him. When he did not return for luncheon she began to worry, fearing some accident, and to make matters worse she fancied she must be coming down with influenza. She felt very sick and thoroughly out of sorts and miserable. She had scarcely touched her breakfast—her uneaten lunch brought an irate Mrs. Melby to see

what ailed her. Fortunately the conversation which
followed did much to hearten both ladies. Mrs.
Melby retired to her own quarters hugging to herself a secret too precious to be shared even with
her husband—at least not just yet—and revolving
plans for making various herbal brews and streng-
thening broths that would ease the little mistress's
discomfort. Fleur, forgetting present misery in
eager planning, waited with growing impatience for
her husband's return, a good deal comforted by Mrs.
Melby's sturdy insistence that if any accident had
befallen him they would surely have heard of it by
now. But the whole afternoon dragged away and
still he did not come. It was barely half an hour
before their early dinner when he as last put in an
appearance, and by that time she was in such a
state of mingled frustration and anxiety that she was
hard put to it to avoid proclaiming her relief in a
thoroughly shrewish scold. Only the fact that his
appearance hardly suggested amorous dalliance
saved him. He was filthy and exhausted—the pallor
over the cheekbones that she had learned to recognise betrayed him—yet somehow he emanated a
secret delight and triumph that she found quite
infuriating.

To add to his sins, having bathed and changed
and eaten a carefully chosen dinner without a word
of comment, he actually fell asleep in front of the
book-room fire. Fleur sat and studied him, relaxed
in the abandonment of sleep, lovingly if crossly.
He looked so much better. One could almost re-

cord his improvement by Mrs. Melby's moods, she mused, smiling. Yesterday the housekeeper had been quite out of temper, rather anxious, when he had rejected the turbot at dinner. She forgot her own annoyance and sat brooding happily over the long supple length of him, sprawled in the chair, until his voice said gently, "Come here, Mrs. Blayden."

She jumped, and stared at him indignantly, remembering all the cause she had for complaint. That was his teasing voice and meant that he was in irrepressible spirits. And he was looking at her with that gleam of grey eyes beneath the sleepy lids that she could never long resist. But tonight she was determined that she would not yield so easily. She tilted her chin at him and remained apparently deaf.

He grinned. This was a game that they had played before. It never lasted long. One or the other of them would start to laugh and Fleur would tumble into his arms to be kissed into submission.

"Chattel!" he said provocatively. And since there was no quiver of response in the cool, prim little face, added wickedly, "Dancing girl! Come! You shall dance for your lord and master!"

There could be no ignoring *that* challenge. She sprang to her feet, eyes sparkling with wrath. "Oh! If only I could! I would show you, I would teach you!"

"What?" A hint of laughter now in the deep lazy voice.

"That my dancing is an art, and no subject for your mocking!"

"Dance for me, then. Behold me most willing to learn of you!"

"You know very well that I can't, not in this dress."

"You could take it off," suggested her tormentor helpfully. "Let—er—art be uninhibited."

She stamped a foot at him furiously. "Yes! I suppose your mistresses that you kept here before me— still keep for all I know—would do just that! But I am your wife. A Blayden. Remember? *I* must behave correctly and respectably, even when my husband neglects me all day and then falls asleep from sheer boredom in my company and insults me and—and—" The fierce tirade ended, predictably, in tears.

He was on his feet in an instant, gathering her close, pouring out his penitence. "My sweet! My little love! Not tears. Please, no! I am a rough, clumsy brute. Forgive me! Indeed I did not mean to mock or to hurt you. Come now. Smile at me! Show me that, in your royal clemency, you will forgive!"

The distress had been real, he thought, smoothing the tear-clotted lashes with gentle lips. Something of more moment than his teasing had provoked it. He had never known her weep before, even in the pain and terror of abduction. Some nonsense about mistresses she had flung at him —but surely she would not reproach him for follies committed when she was still in the schoolroom? Her sense of fairness was one of the qualities that so endeared her to him. Nevertheless there was some trouble here that must be probed.

The storm of sobbing was done. She lay lax and biddable against him. "And what is all this nonsense about my mistresses?" he said gently. "A shocking imputation to fling at a devoted husband! I'd have you know, ma'am, that I, too, am a Blayden and must comport myself with due propriety. I've never so much as thought of keeping a mistress here. Why! It is my home."

There was something about the simplicity of that last phrase that carried far more conviction than any vehement protest. Fleur opened tear-swollen eyes—she was not one of those favoured creatures who can cry prettily—and looked at him with an expression of mingled doubt and hope. "But everyone said—" she faltered.

"What everyone says is generally exaggerated if not wholly false," said her husband bracingly, "but tell me, just the same."

Thus encouraged the whole story came tumbling out, from what Melly had told her before they had even met to Papa-Paul's condemnation and even the sentimental recollections of Rose's friend. On her childish lips it made a shocking indictment. He took his time over answering it since he felt that he owed her complete honesty yet wished to present his case in its most favourable aspect.

"I was twenty when I was first cast upon the

Town," he began quietly. "There *were* affairs—
of a fleeting, casual nature, perfectly understood
by both parties, just as I also tried my luck at
gaming and on the race course. I can assure you
that very soon it became a dead bore. And it was
never suffered to intrude on my real life, here, after
I had inherited Dakers from my uncle. The story
of the 'ravishing mistress' that I keep in seclusion
here"—he quoted Papa-Paul's phrase with a wry
grimace—"is pure fabrication."

He hesitated briefly. This was delicate ground.
Though the need for absolute secrecy was happily
over, long training had made him reluctant to dis-
close more than was absolutely necessary. "Because
of my knowledge of France and my fluency of the
language," he said carefully, "it was decided that
I could make myself useful by crossing the channel
from time to time and bringing back first hand news
of what was happening over there. My reputation
for—er—gallantry was turned to good account. The
stories about my glamorous inamorata were put
about deliberately to cover my absences."

Fleur had noticed his wariness; had, in fact, already had some inkling of the truth, since it was the
only explanation that fitted the facts. So. Now she
knew exactly what he had been doing in Fleurus.
Guessed, too, that it was knowledge that he would
gladly keep from her. Her throat felt thick and
aching from recent tears and present thankfulness,
but somehow she found a placid, almost disin-
terested voice, somehow preserved an innocent front

as she said, "So that is how it was. I *do* wish you had told me sooner."

She knew that he was not wholly deceived. Such childish ignorance, such crass stupidity, must always be suspect. Luckily distraction was ready to her hand. "Then where have you been all day, if you have not been with a mistress?" she demanded severely.

He hugged her so hard that it hurt, and said solemnly, "But I *have* been with a mistress. One that had held me in thrall these three years past. Today she was delivered of a fine son. I had meant to introduce you, but she was shy, you know, understandably in the circumstances—"

At this point the indignant Fleur, perfectly well aware by the tight tuck in his cheek and the heavings of suppressed mirth that he was trying to fool her in most outrageous fashion, sat up erect on his lap and said sweetly, "Pray describe her to me, this nonpareil among females. Golden hair, I suppose, and big blue eyes?"

"They *are* very large," he agreed judicially. "But not blue. Brown. A tender, melting brown."

"Like toffee," suggested his wife helpfully.

He choked slightly but went on, "And I would describe her as chestnut rather than golden. A rich, glowing chestnut. While as for her legs! So slender, so— But I suppose it would be indelicate in me to describe *them* in detail."

"Since I strongly suspect that she had four of them, you may do so with my very good will," retorted his wife. "Now do stop funning, Marc, and tell me properly. It's a new foal, isn't it? Why didn't you tell me? And why haven't I so much as set eyes on the mother?"

He settled her more comfortably against him, stretching out long legs luxuriously towards the glowing hearth and sighing his content as he began to explain.

The uncle who had bequeathed him Dakers had been interested in breeding racehorses and at the time of his death had owned several brood mares and some promising youngsters. Marc, lacking the resources to finance so expensive and chancy a venture, had sold them and used their price to rehabilitate the farmland and buildings and improve the quality of his stock. It was dull work, perhaps, in comparison with breeding horses, but he liked it, and it paid steady dividends, if not handsome ones. Three years ago he had permitted himself the luxury of buying a yearling filly, Sweet Sorrel, bred out of one of the Dakars' mares.

"She's rising four now," he told Fleur, "and it's her first foal. She's a nervous creature so we kept her away from the bustle and noise of the home stable. Job has her down at his place. It wouldn't do for her to be upset by strangers—especially jealous females," he threw in teasingly. "In a few days, when she has really accepted the foal, you may see my charmer for yourself. The foal's a beauty. Dark Plantagenet is his sire. Good blood lines there. This youngster should have both staying power and a pretty turn of speed. You may amuse yourself by choosing a name for him, because he is yours, sweetheart, my Christmas gift to you. I had meant to keep my secret till Christmas Day, but trust a wife to give one no peace until she knows the whole."

She caught one of his hands and carried it to her cheek, rubbing herself lovingly against it. "You are so good to me, Marc. So much too good. And I can give you nothing in return. Not even Grandpapa's money," she added regretfully, "which you had every right to expect."

The hand that she was fondling twisted to cup her chin and turn her face to his. His expression was grave. "Do you really not understand what you have given me, beloved?" he said quietly.

It was the first time that he had ever called her so. She savoured it so joyously that she missed a good deal of his following remarks, which was a pity since they were both eloquent and sincere, an unusual combination. However, the bit that she *did* hear was eminently satisfactory.

"—a home," said the reflective voice. "A place where a man can be at ease and always confident of support and sympathy. And laughter, too, for that is more important than I had dreamed, while even a well-deserved scolding is comforting in its way. At least it assures me that my wife prefers my conversation to my snores! As for the money—we shall do very well as we are. And perhaps Sweet Sorrel's son will make another fortune for you.

Master Robert Pennington Blayden may have your grandfather's and we will make Blayden a happier home for him than ever it was for Deb and me. And talking of happy homes, since you have wrested half of my secret from me I may as well confess the whole. We are to expect guests for Christmas. Is your housekeeping equal to the imposition? No—not Deb. My father thinks it too risky for her, since the northern roads are already partly snowbound, though he says she may come to us in the better weather. I saw him when I was in Town last week. However, *your* family are less chicken hearted. *They* are prepared to accept the risk of being marooned indefinitely in darkest Kent in order to assure themselves that all is well with their darling."

He was scarcely permitted to finish. She flung her arms about his neck and hugged him vigorously. "Truly? All of them? That will make Christmas quite perfect. Not that it wouldn't be very much nicer if we could be just by ourselves," she added, a sample of feminine logic which made her husband smile even while he perfectly understood her sentiments.

"I thought you would be pleased," he told her. "I was a trifle anxious about M. Lavelle's response to my invitation after the trick I served him, but he seems to have taken it in good part. I have arranged to bring them down on Thursday and they will be with us a sennight at least. And next, I suppose, you will wish to go jauntering off to London."

It was half statement, half question. Fleur accepted it gravely, along with the implication that the period of her probation was over.

"You did promise that you would hire a house in Town and that I should go to all the fashionable parties," she reminded him demurely.

"I did," he agreed. He did not find the prospect particularly enticing, but if that was what she wanted, she should have it.

"But there is always the danger that someone might recognise the notorious Madame Flora," she went on, "and since it is only six months since Grandpapa died I could not go to parties anyway. So perhaps we had better just stay quietly at Dakers."

Marc having expressed wholehearted approval of this sensible suggestion, Fleur said, "We might go up to Town for a week or two in the spring. I know of a very good hotel that Mr. Willets told me of, and I shall have lots of shopping to do by then."

"Shopping?" groaned her husband. "Extravagant little wretch! Why! You've not worn the half of the gowns I bought you but two months since!"

"Nevertheless I shall need new ones in the spring," she told him firmly. "And permit me to inform you, sir, that your knowledge of feminine needs in the way of apparel, and more particularly of underwear and nightrail, is entirely reprehensible."

He chuckled. "But you like wearing them, don't you, love! And will be glad of my advice when it comes to choosing more?"

She laughed, but shook her head. "To speak truth I was not thinking of clothes when I spoke of shopping," she said slowly.

"What, then?" he asked indulgently.

She was silent for a minute. Then she said, "I want you to buy me a horse."

There was lively surprise in his face. "A horse, child? With half a dozen in the stables already, and generally too fresh to handle because they're not worked hard enough? And a brand new foal awaiting your inspection. Not that you'll be able to ride *him* of course. What kind of a horse?"

She turned her face into his breast so that her voice was muffled. He heard her say, shyly. "Perhaps it is too soon to be making plans—but Mrs. Melby is sure it is so, and indeed I think so myself. I want you to buy me a new rocking horse for the nursery at Blayden."

A REGENCY ROMANCE

BY CLAUDETTE WILLIAMS

SPRING GAMBIT   2-3025-2 $1.50

Nicole Beaumont was the joy and despair of every eligible
London gentleman. Her first social season was a smashing
success. The high-spirited beauty enchanted every young man
she met, but she wanted only one—Adam Roth, Duke of
Lyndham. When Nicky announced she was going to marry
for love, unlike many in her set, Adam didn't know that he
was her target.

SPRING GAMBIT—A joyous adventure in Regency England
with a heroine who throws convention to the winds and her
heart to the man she loves.

THE ROMANTIC FRENCHMAN

by Mary Ann Gibbs

P2869 $1.25

Lady Tamporley had almost forgotten what romance had been like. At age 26, she was a pretty and gentle matron with five children. Sarah was quite content and expected her future to be much the same as her past.

Then the handsome French Lieutenant, Philippe Cadot, suddenly came into her life. Philippe, a gallant and charming prisoner of war on parole in England, was everything her loud and pompous husband was not.

Philippe was as enchanted with Sarah as she was with him. And in the brief and gentle days of springtime their love blossomed.

Her heart and thoughts were with Philippe, while she continued to go through the motions of being Lady Tamporley. For now, she refused to think that their affair could ever come to an end. . . .